Peril at
PIRATE'S POINT
Lee Roddy

PUBLISHING
Colorado Springs, Colorado

PERIL AT PIRATE'S POINT
Copyright © 1993 by Lee Roddy

CIP Data

Published by Focus on the Family Publishing, Colorado Springs, Colorado 80903
Distributed by Word Books, Dallas, Texas.

Editor: Ron Klug
Cover Illustration: Ernest Norica
Cover Design: James A. Lebbad

Printed in the United States of America

93 94 95 96 97 98/ 10 9 8 7 6 5 4 3 2 1

CONTENTS

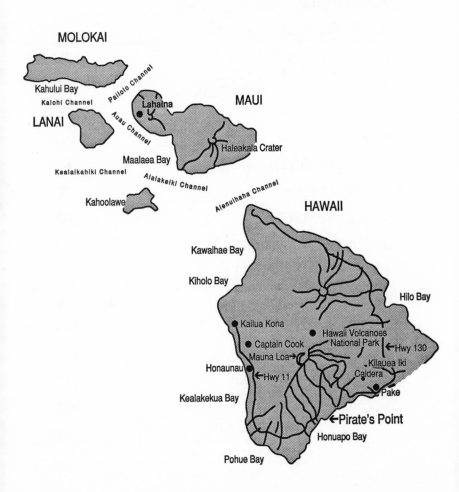

Pacific Ocean

MOLOKAI

Kahului Bay

Kalohi Channel

Pailolo Channel

Lahaina

MAUI

LANAI

Auau Channel

Haleakala Crater

Maalaea Bay

Kealaikahiki Channel

Alalakeiki Channel

Kahoolawe

Alenuihaha Channel

HAWAII

Kawaihae Bay

Kiholo Bay

Hilo Bay

Kailua Kona

Hawaii Volcanoes
National Park

←Hwy 130

Captain Cook

Mauna Loa→

Kilauea Iki

Honaunau

Caldera

←Hwy 11

Pake

Kealakekua Bay

←Pirate's Point

Honuapo Bay

Pohue Bay

Chapter One

PLANE DOWN AT SEA

Josh Ladd gulped hard, staring at the motionless propeller on the right wing. He glanced toward his best friend sitting beside him on the left. Tank Catlett gazed fearfully out his window at the second engine, which sputtered and threatened to stop. Josh's blue eyes flicked to Tank's father, piloting the rented twin-engine plane low over the Pacific Ocean.

Sam Catlett, sitting directly in front of his son, pulled back hard on the yoke, desperately trying to keep the nose up on the two-engine craft. He raised his voice above the noise of the remaining engine and its propeller spinning silvery circles in the clear Hawaiian air. "You boys see anything?"

"No, not on this side," Josh answered, forcing his eyes back to the water. He again wildly searched the surface for a boat that might come to their aid when they ditched the aircraft in the three-foot swells. He saw only the vast empty expanse of deep blue water stretching to the horizon off the

1

Big Island of Hawaii.

"Nothing on this side between here and those cliffs," Tank replied. He usually spoke in a slow, unhurried way. But now his voice was high with fright, and his words were rushed.

"Keep looking!" Mr. Catlett urged. "I think I can coax her around that point. Then we're going in. Tank, you check for a beach or someplace where we can swim ashore."

Josh again glanced at Tank. His straight, blond hair was bleached almost white from the sun. Under his orange life jacket, he wore an old green tee shirt, faded cutoffs, and hiking boots.

Josh swallowed hard, looking beyond his friend to the high, rugged, black volcanic cliffs visible out the left window. They had loomed menacingly off the port wing since the pilot turned out to sea after the engine quit over the erupting volcano. The surface of the ocean offered the only possible place for a crash landing.

Josh stole a fearful glance down at the waves. They rose ponderously from a submerged coral reef and raced shoreward in blue-green splendor. They exploded furiously against the base of the cliffs, shattered into white foam, and fell back into the sea.

"Josh," Tank's father said over his shoulder, "you'd better crack that door a little so it won't get smashed and trap us inside when we hit the water. And keep looking for anyone who could help us."

Fighting his anxiety, Josh nodded and obeyed. As he

unlatched the only door and slid it back slightly, the air rushed noisily inside. He looked down at the ocean now less than 30 feet below. It seemed to be rushing up to meet the stricken aircraft.

The waters were so clear that Josh glimpsed the wrecks of two old ships on the bottom, but he barely noticed as he anxiously scanned the surface ahead. As they slowly rounded a mountainous point of land, he hoped to see a ship, a boat, or at least a windsurfer who might help them when they splashed down.

Suddenly Tank exclaimed, "Dad, there's a beach!"

Josh swiveled his head to the left, feeling his orange life jacket lightly scratch his chin as he again looked beyond Tank to the shore. All Josh could see was the base of the soaring cliffs and great sprays of foam as the waves struck the shore.

"I see it," Mr. Catlett said, kicking the rudder around sharply so the left wing dipped. "It's mighty small, but it'll have to do. Hang on! I'm going to try getting her beyond the reef and set her down close enough so we can swim to shore. Be sure your seat belts and shoulder harnesses are tight."

Josh checked the harness strap that ran across his left shoulder and buckled to the lap belt on the right. He gulped fearfully, said a quick, silent prayer, and watched in dread as the craft leveled out and sank rapidly toward the whitecaps now directly below. He braced his hiking boots firmly on the floor, bending forward in his old, red aloha shirt and faded blue jeans until his stiff life jacket stopped his movement.

Tank's father called over his shoulder, "When we stop moving, get out fast. Try to stay together!"

Josh nodded numbly. Out of the corner of his eye, he saw the point of land slide slowly by.

Suddenly Tank cried, "Look! There's a power boat with a man in it near the beach! See?"

"I see him!" Tank's father replied. "And he sees us! He's looking up at us. I'll try to pancake in as close to him as possible so he can pick us up."

Tank's shoulders blocked Josh's view.

Suddenly Tank stiffened. "Hey, he's not waiting! He's heading for shore. See his wake? He's speeded up, going wide open away from us!"

Josh couldn't believe that, but before he could say anything, Mr. Catlett called out sharply. "Brace yourselves!"

Josh took a deep breath just as the plane slammed down hard. It skidded forward, rocking violently as Mr. Catlett tried to keep the nose up. But as the aircraft lost speed, the heavy front portion dipped sharply.

Josh felt the plane spin crazily. Then the lighter tail end suddenly flipped up and forward. Josh was thrown violently against his lap belt and shoulder harness. He had a momentary sensation of being spun around. The plane came to rest facing the direction they'd come. The door ripped off and sea water rushed into the cabin.

"You okay, Tank?" Josh asked.

"I think so." Tank's voice quavered as he unsnapped his

shoulder harness. "Dad?"

Sam Catlett slumped over the yoke, unconscious, as the water poured into the cabin.

"Dad!"

"Let's get him out of here!" Josh cried, fumbling with the seat belt.

As the buckles fell free, both boys splashed through the water surging into the cabin. They reached Tank's father at the same instant.

The plane's heavy engines forced the craft down fast. The boys worked quickly to release the unconscious man from his seat.

"Grab hold of him!" Josh urged, seizing Mr. Catlett under the armpits from the back. "Let's get him out of here before we all go under!"

Tank's father was a tall, thin man, but he proved to be all that both boys could handle. They dragged him out of his seat while Josh fought off a sense of panic as the water surged noisily up to his knees.

With a sudden downward lurch, the plane started slowly slipping nose first beneath the surface.

"We're going down!" Tank cried.

"We have to get him out now!" Josh yelled, pulling mightily on the unconscious man, whose upper body slid toward the door, then suddenly stopped.

"His foot must be caught!" Josh exclaimed. "Keep his head up! I'll free it." Josh dropped to his knees and felt below the water, which was now up to his waist. "His boot's caught between the rudder pedals and the fire wall!" he cried. "I can't move his foot!"

"Let me try!" Tank plunged his face into the water.

Josh's mind screamed a warning, *Get out! Save yourselves!* But Josh couldn't do that. He took a quick breath and wordlessly plunged his face into the rising waters beside Tank.

The ocean off of Hawaii is amazingly clear. But the roiled waters in the cabin were so filled with bubbles that Josh could see only the outline of the trapped foot and Tank's fingers trying to free his father.

The buoyant life jacket tended to lift Josh toward the cabin roof as the cabin rapidly filled with water. Josh grabbed the yoke with one hand in order to stay down. He kept his eyes open in spite of the stinging seawater and helped in the frenzied efforts to release the foot.

There! I think we're getting it...oh!

His thoughts were snapped off as the plane lurched sideways. Josh's fingers were torn from the boot. Josh's head popped up above the water which had now nearly filled the cabin. He sucked in gulps of air and glanced out the door.

Through the little space that remained above water, Josh glimpsed the steep cliffs now barely a hundred yards away. The power boat was still racing toward shore. There the surf crashed against the sheer cliffs and washed more gently across a small black-sand beach.

Why doesn't he come help us? Josh's thought was ripped away as the plane sank steadily. He took a quick breath and fought the life jacket's upward tug. Josh returned to try freeing the trapped foot.

He held onto the yoke with both hands, jackknifed, and thrust his boot soles against the fire wall. He shoved with all his strength while Tank struggled with his father's foot. Suddenly, Mr. Catlett's life jacket shot him to the ceiling.

There! He's free! Josh's joyous thought was followed with another frightening one. *He's been under an awfully long time. Got to get him to the surface!*

Fighting an urgent need to breathe, Josh helped Tank drag the limp man through the door. The life jackets propelled them 20 feet to the surface.

There Josh sucked in a great breath of fresh air, facing Tank across his unconscious father.

"He's not breathing!" Tank cried.

Both boys had learned mouth-to-mouth resuscitation before moving from California to Hawaii. Josh knew that speed was now essential to restart breathing. He had practiced such resuscitation in shallow water, but couldn't do that while bouncing in three-foot swells.

Josh shouted, "We have to get him ashore, fast! The life jacket will keep his face out of the water."

Tank groaned in anguish and gripped his father's life jacket near the shoulder. Josh grabbed the other side, then began stroking rapidly with his free hand. Tank did the same.

"Look, he's bleeding!" Tank moaned, staring at the dark stain drifting up to the surface.

"Probably cut on the coral. Come on, swim!"

As another wave crested, Josh saw that the boat he'd seen earlier had disappeared. *Where'd he go? Why didn't he come to help us?*

Everything became a blur of time for Josh. Far overhead, he saw the fluffy white clouds floating in from the sea toward the volcano still erupting out of sight inland. Waves rushing shoreward helped propel the survivors toward shore.

It all looked so peaceful, yet Josh knew that tragedy was at hand. *He couldn't have been under the water more than a minute, if that long. But by the time we get him to shallow water where we can give him mouth-to-mouth resuscitation, it may be too late!*

Josh was jarred out of his musings as a huge wave caught him. He twisted his head to see that they were almost to the beach. He started to lower his feet, hoping to feel the bottom. At the same instant, he felt himself being sucked under.

He managed to take a quick breath of air before the wave crashed over him, tearing his grip from the unconscious pilot. Josh tumbled violently under the water, helpless as a pebble. He heard the roar of the surf and the surging of bubbles. He felt himself carried toward the shore with jet-plane speed.

Josh could tell from the brightness above him that he was on his back. He tried to stroke upward, only to feel himself lifted as by a giant hand. When his head broke free of the water, he gulped air, his face to the sun. Then the wave ceased its forward motion, collapsed on the sand, and retreated, leaving Josh three feet up in the air.

He dropped on his back with such force that the wind was knocked out of him. For a moment he lay stunned. He was only vaguely aware of the gentle, warm trade winds on his face and the black volcanic sand grinding into his bare legs, his arms, and the back of his head.

As his senses returned, Josh sat up. He was relieved to see Tank nearby, brushing sand from his scraped elbows. Tank's father lay face down on the black sand, his right leg seeping blood onto his wet pants. Both his feet swung limply as the waves rushed in.

Josh scrambled to his feet, his boots sloshing with water. "You okay, Tank?"

"I think so." Tank turned to his father. "Dad?"

Josh ran to the unconscious man and helped Tank roll him over. Tank began mouth-to-mouth resuscitation.

Come on, Mr. Catlett! Josh thought. *Breathe!* He switched to a silent, anguished prayer, *O Lord, help us save him!*

As the trade winds dried the salt on his skin, Josh began to despair. *It's too late!* He shook off the thought, replacing it with another: *"Trust in the..."*

"He's breathing!" Tank interrupted joyfully, straightening up. "Let's get him into the recovery position, fast!"

As Josh started to help, he suddenly stiffened at the startled expression on Tank's face. "What's the matter?"

"Look!"

Josh followed Tank's gaze. A shirtless man scowled at the boys from a crevice in the cliff at the far end of the little beach. He had a flaming red beard, a blue bandanna on his head, and a black patch over his left eye. A brightly colored parrot perched on his right shoulder.

He stood on his right leg, supported by a crude crutch under his left armpit. From his tattered shorts, a wooden leg extended from his left knee to the ground. A cutlass gleamed in his right hand.

Josh blinked in surprise, feeling as though they'd stumbled into a time warp or a time machine.

"Avast thar, ye swabs!" the wild-looking stranger roared, brandishing the weapon menacingly over his head. "I know ye be after Captain Kidd's treasure, so now ye'll have to walk the plank!"

"Look, mister," Josh began, indicating the pilot who was stirring but hadn't tried to sit up. "He needs..."

"Mutiny, is it?" the one-legged man thundered, lowering the cutlass toward Josh. He took a hobbling step, shouting, "The plank's too good fer the likes of ye! Now ye'll taste this blade!"

Chapter Two

THE PIRATE AND THE BUSH VETS

For a moment Josh looked anxiously at the wild-eyed pirate who hobbled awkwardly forward, slashing the cutlass in silvery circles. Josh was reminded of Long John Silver in Robert Louis Stevenson's *Treasure Island*. There hadn't been any real pirates in hundreds of years, but this one-legged man with the gleaming blade seemed to be one.

Tank whispered, "Do you think he's serious?"

"He looks serious to me."

"Well, do something while I take care of my dad!" Tank quickly raised his father's near arm above his head as the first step in the drowning recovery position.

Josh nodded and glanced hopefully around for a piece of driftwood or anything that might serve as a defensive weapon. The black-sand beach offered nothing at all.

An idea hit Josh. He slipped out of his life jacket and draped it quickly over his left arm. It offered partial protection from the steel blade. Thrusting his arm out in front of him, but staying out of reach of the flashing cutlass, Josh again

11

called to the advancing man.

"Look, mister, we don't mean any harm! Our plane went down and had to come ashore here. We need help ..."

"No swabs the likes of ye steals Captain Kidd's treasure!" the one-legged man shouted from less than twenty feet away. "Stand whar ye be!"

Josh thought of a second possibility. "Tank," he said, lowering his voice, "if he keeps coming, I'll try to knock the sword out of his hand with this jacket. If I can't do that, I'll use it to sweep the crutch out from under him. I'd hate to do that, but I'd hate even more for him to cut us up!"

Quickly Josh gripped one end of his life jacket and started swinging the other. "Mister, if you don't stop. . ."

The pirate interrupted, "Ye'll be shark bait after ye taste my steel, boy!" He turned away from Tank and his father, jabbing the cutlass toward Josh.

Josh licked his lips and retreated, trying to draw the pirate farther away from the Catletts. Out of the corner of his eye, Josh saw that Tank had removed his life jacket and crossed his father's far arm over his chest in the second drowning recovery step. Tank then bent his father's bleeding leg at the knee, gripped his clothing at the hip and pulled him toward himself.

Josh's eyes flickered back to the pirate just as something moved at a crevice behind him. "Tank!" Josh cried hoarsely. "There's another one!"

The second man wore combat boots, an old, olive-drab

undershirt, and faded cutoff shorts of the same color. He had a a black beard and long stringy hair with gray streaks in both. He cradled a modern military assault rifle in the crook of his left arm.

"You heard the captain," he said sternly. "Stand still! Drop that life jacket!"

As Josh reluctantly obeyed, the one-legged man stopped less than ten feet away. Josh decided that the second man sounded rational. "Hi!" Josh called. "Our plane went down and..."

"I saw it," the new arrival interrupted, catching up with the one-legged pirate. "Begging your pardon, sir," the rifleman said politely to the man with the cutlass. "I'll take them off your hands if you'd like."

For a moment, the man who called himself Captain Kidd scowled as though thinking about that. "Very well, Mr. Hook," he said finally, lowering the weapon. "Throw them in irons. I'll deal with them later."

"Whew!" Josh said to the man with the rifle. "Thank you!"

"Shut up, kid!" he replied sharply.

The pirate dropped his crutch and sank awkwardly onto the sand. This caused the parrot to squawk and flutter to keep its balance on the man's shoulder. "Mr. Hook," the pirate said, his voice softening and the wildness going out of his eyes, "I'll make myself more comfortable before retiring to my quarters."

Josh blinked in surprise as the man placed his cutlass on the sand. He removed the black eye patch, revealing two perfectly good blue eyes. Next, he began unbuckling some leather straps above his peg leg, which fell onto the beach. Josh's mouth dropped open in amazement as the man slowly straightened out the rest of the leg. It must have been bent at the knee and tied to his thigh behind him.

He stood on both good legs and swept the bandanna away from his head. Although he wasn't any older than Tank's father, this man was totally bald except for a small half circle of reddish-gold hair from his ears back. He grinned broadly at the boys, who exchanged startled glances.

"Surprised, are you?" he asked, obviously pleased with himself. "Well, more surprises are ahead." His speech and manner had totally changed. He spoke with quiet authority. "Sergeant, please render first aid to that man. When he's able to walk, escort him and these young gentlemen to my headquarters."

"Yes, sir!" the man now called sergeant replied. He saluted smartly with his right hand. "Right away."

Totally confused, Josh watched as the man with the parrot picked up his peg leg and cutlass. He walked easily to the crevice where he had first been seen. He pushed some heavy green foliage aside, revealing an entrance in the face of the cliff. He squeezed through. The foliage dropped back into place, totally hiding the opening.

Josh and Tank exchanged bewildered glances before the

sergeant unexpectedly thrust the rifle into Josh's hands. "Hold this," he said bruskly, "while I see what we can do for your friend."

In his surprise, Josh nearly dropped the strange weapon. He had never seen one, except on television, and had no idea how it worked. He gingerly hung on to the rifle as the sergeant knelt beside Sam Catlett.

Tank's father tried to sit up. "I'm ... I'm okay," he said weakly. "Just got a headache. Must've hit my. . . "

"Don't talk!" the sergeant broke in. "Just lie quietly and let me have a good look at you. Boys, step back and give him plenty of air."

Josh and Tank obeyed while Mr. Catlett lay down and closed his eyes with a soft sigh. When his life jacket was removed, he appeared even more slender and wiry than Josh remembered.

Josh glanced at the sergeant's throat where he wore a small chain with two metal tags. Josh lowered his voice so only Tank could see. "See those military dog tags around his neck? I noticed the other fellow had some like it. He also had a shark's tooth."

"So?" Tank asked absently, watching his father.

"I think maybe we've stumbled into some of those bush vets.* You know: those Vietnam war veterans who still live in the jungles around Hawaii."

Tank stared. "You mean like those your father interviewed for his newspaper?"

"Yes. Many of them returned to the jungles to escape the stresses of civilized life. But a few had their mental circuits burned out from taking powerful drugs in Vietnam."

Tank's eyes widened in understanding. "Some of them are crazy, really pupule!"*

Josh agreed. "Yes, but not all. Some bush vets just don't like to be around other people. But if these two men really are crazy, we're in big trouble!"

"Well," Tank whispered back hopefully, "this one's helping my dad. Maybe that's a good sign."

I hope so! Josh told himself fervently.

After what appeared to be a brief but expert examination of Tank's father, the rifleman grunted in satisfaction and stood up.

Josh asked, "What do you think?"

"He's got a bad bump on his head and a possible concussion. But he's breathing okay."

"Thank God!" Josh whispered.

"What about his leg?" Tank asked. "It's still bleeding."

"Coral cut, I think," the sergeant answered. "That's probably the worst thing that's happened to him. A piece of the living coral might have broken off in the wound. Infection could set in."

Josh nodded, remembering the terrible-looking wound one of his young friends in Honolulu had suffered after a coral cut. "We have to get him to a doctor fast!"

The sergeant shook his head. "Sorry, boys." He retrieved the rifle, which Josh had held gingerly and with a certain amount of dread. "No doctors around here."

"Then call for one!" Tank cried. "He's my father!"

"No telephones or radios here, either," the sergeant replied. "We'll do what we can for him back at camp."

"When we don't come home," Josh protested, "my parents and Tank's mother will have the Coast Guard looking for us. We could watch for them and signal..."

"Forget it, boys!" The sergeant reached down and pulled Tank's father to his feet. "I'm Dick Tanner. What's your name?"

"Catlett. Sam Catlett." He brushed the sand off his right hand and shook with Tanner. "Thanks for your help. Oh, this is my son, Tank, and his best friend, Josh Ladd. Mr. Tanner, why can't the boys stay here and signal a search plane when it flies over?"

"I'll let the lieutenant explain that," Tanner answered gruffly. "Come on. Let's not keep him waiting!"

Tank said, "I thought he called himself Captain Kidd?"

Tanner shrugged. "Sometimes he's Captain Kidd, the pirate. Sometimes he's the lieutenant. Let's move!"

He strode purposefully across the black sand. Josh and Tank followed, walking on each side of Tank's limping father. Their guide pulled the foliage aside where the first man had disappeared.

Josh exclaimed in surprise at what he saw. "A lava tube!"* It was about five feet high and as wide.

Tank's father said quietly, "There are lots of lava tubes on these islands."

Josh nodded, remembering others he'd seen. Most were quite small, but he'd heard of the big Thurston Lava Tube not far from Kilauea Iki* All such tubes had been made long ago when the molten lava from an erupting volcano cooled faster on the outside. However, the inner magma had continued flowing until it had entirely drained out, leaving a hollow tube.

Josh had to bend his head only a little to walk through this one, but the two men had to stoop nearly double. After about a hundred feet the tube ended, and everyone stepped into another world.

They were in a small pocket valley totally surrounded on all sides by mountain peaks. Ahead of them stretched a jungle not unlike those of the Koolau Range* behind the capital city at Honolulu. This rain forest of great trees was heavily festooned with fruit and flowers. Immense vines trailed long tendrils toward the ground.

Above the tree tops, white cumulus clouds floated under the bright sun. There was no hint that the Pacific Ocean was close by. The mountains totally cut off any sight or sound of the sea. It was the most remote, primitive area of Hawaii Josh had seen.

"Where are we?" Josh asked their guide as they followed a narrow trail toward a magnificent waterfall. It fell like a silver ribbon, gracefully cascading 500 or 600 feet straight down before bouncing off a ledge. A fine mist like an immense spider's web caught countless rainbows that flitted about like beautiful butterflies. From the bottom of the mist, the stream emerged and plunged downward again for another 200 feet.

"We call it Pirate's Point," Tanner replied over his shoulder. He added sharply, "Stay on the trail."

"Why?" Tank asked innocently.

"Because you could get hurt if you stepped off of it, that's why," the guide answered bluntly.

Josh looked in puzzlement at Tank, who shrugged.

Sam Catlett said in a low voice, "Better do as he says, boys. Josh, do you remember what your father wrote about how some marijuana growers protect their crops?"

Josh understood. He glanced at Tank, whose eyes showed he also understood about pokololo,* as the illegal plant was known in the islands. John Ladd, in his recent interviews with the bush vets, had learned that some marijuana growers protected their illegal patches with deadly tricks they had learned in Vietnam many years ago. That included deadly punji sticks* hidden in the grass that could inflict terrible leg and foot injuries.

Josh shuddered at the thought of what could happen to an unwary person who might discover this area. He made sure he stayed well in the middle of the narrow trail. He asked no more questions; by now he was sure that the captors were dangerous.

After some slow walking because of Mr. Catlett's leg injury, they entered a clearing. Four military tents stood beneath the spreading shelter of an immense monkey pod tree.

Josh frowned. *Four tents? Must be more than just these two bush vets living here.*

In a common open area, there was an outdoor cooking space, a 50-gallon drum that Josh guessed contained drinking water, and a hammock swung between two trees. The parrot that had been perched on the pirate's shoulder walked awkwardly along a crude wooden table with benches.

Sounds, like those in a zoo, attracted Josh's attention. Beyond the living area, he saw wire cages of various sizes. They were tucked under low-growing vines and trees. Josh glimpsed one caged dog and several cats. From beyond their cages Josh heard the squawking of exotic birds and caught a flash of brilliant reds and greens as they flew inside a six-foot-high wire enclosure.

The dog barked shrilly at the new arrivals until the man with the rifle yelled, "Shut up, Maka!"

The dog, a skinny, black, mixed breed, retreated silently to the back of his cage.

The lieutenant stepped out of the nearest tent. He motioned for the visitors to sit at the table. All three obeyed, but the man remained standing. He eyed Sam Catlett and the boys thoughtfully.

"I'm Ross Beacher, formerly second lieutenant in the U.S. Army," he began with no hint of the pirate character he had assumed earlier. "I see you've met Sergeant Tanner. We served together in 'Nam."*

Tank's father, favoring his cut leg, briefly introduced himself to Beacher and extended his right hand. Beacher ignored it. Mr. Catlett slowly withdrew his hand. Ignoring the rebuff, he introduced the boys, then explained their situation.

"We were flying over the volcano to see the eruption when we lost an engine. So I turned out to sea, looking for a ship or someone to pick us up, but..."

"I know," Beacher interrupted. "We saw you."

Suddenly Josh thought of the boat and the single occupant who had disappeared instead of waiting to rescue them when they splashed down. Josh stared thoughtfully at Sergeant Tanner.

I think he's the man in the boat! That realization made Josh extremely concerned, because something was terribly wrong here. Josh tried to ignore the warning bells clanging inside his head.

"Mr. Beacher..." Tank's father began, but was again interrupted.

"Lieutenant Beacher," the man corrected.

Mr. Catlett nodded. "Lieutenant Beacher, our families will be worried sick when we don't return. I'd appreciate it if you'd let them know..."

"They'll just have to worry," Beacher broke in. He added bluntly, "You see, I can't let any of you go."

"What?" Josh exclaimed.

"That's right!" Beacher snapped, shaking his head emphatically. "I can't let any of you leave this place ... ever!"

Chapter Three

THE GIRL WITH THE SNAKE

A few minutes later Josh fought panic at the idea that they could never go home again. He had joined Tank and his father in arguing with Beacher, but it had been useless. Now, at Beacher's orders, Josh and Tank followed Tanner with his rifle through the clearing, past the caged birds and animals, and into the jungle.

"I can't believe it!" Josh exclaimed in a hoarse whisper so Tanner couldn't overhear. "There's no way we're going to spend the rest of our lives here."

"Well, that's what Lieutenant Beacher said, although he wouldn't say why."

"We can guess why. Marijuana growers don't want anybody telling the police where their pot* is growing."

Tank glanced suspiciously ahead at Tanner carrying his rifle. "Sometimes they don't leave any witnesses. Do you think he's taking us into the jungle to...?"

"No!" Josh broke in. "Stop scaring yourself. Remember that the lieutenant told the sergeant to lead us to Pua* and

Keoni,* whoever they are."

"They must part of this gang of pokololo growers."

"Could be. Pua means flower, I think. So maybe she's the wife of one of these men."

"I know a kid in Honolulu named Keoni," Tank said. "It's Hawaiian for John." Tank looked hopefully at Josh. "If we're not being led into the jungle to die, then how come the sergeant left us all to drown when he saw us from his boat when our plane was going down?"

"I don't know," Josh admitted. "Unless that pupule lieutenant wanted us alive for some other reason."

"I guess they could have left us on the beach if they'd wanted," Tank mused.

"That's right. Without food or water, we'd never have survived unless the Coast Guard found us fast."

"Maybe they brought us here, away from the beach, so the Coast Guard couldn't find us. Boy! Whatever reason they have, you know that lieutenant has got to really be pupule! I mean, dressing up like a pirate and trying to stick us with his sword."

"Did you see how fast his whole personality changed from pirate to bush vet? It's like he's two different persons. I wonder how this man puts up with him?" Josh glanced toward Tanner.

"Maybe it has something to do with when they were both soldiers in Vietnam."

"Whatever it is, I'm sorry we're in this mess," Josh said.

"None of us could help it that the plane went down."

"I know, but we can't spend the rest of our lives here! We've got to escape or call for help."

"How are we going to do that?" Tank asked.

Josh looked ahead to make sure Tanner couldn't overhear. "Well, we know your father put a May Day distress call out on the radio before we went down. So the Coast Guard will know our location at that time."

Tank brightened. "Yeah, they'll send searchers out and maybe they'll see our plane in that shallow water."

"Yes, but they'd never find the lava tube that leads into this place. And if they fly over, they won't be able to see under these jungle trees. So we'll have to escape on our own."

"How?"

"Well," Josh said, thinking fast, "we can't walk out because of your father's injuries..."

"I hope he doesn't get an infection," Tank interrupted, "even though Mr. Tanner washed Dad's cut with soap and water and poured vinegar on it. That's what the divers and surfers do when they get a coral cut."

Josh nodded in agreement. *I just hope Mr. Catlett doesn't have a concussion or something more than a bump on his head,* he thought. *No sense in saying that to Tank. It'd just worry him.*

Aloud, Josh said, "We might escape in the boat we saw Sergeant Tanner using when we crashed."

"Yeah! Good idea! Where do you suppose he hid it?"

"I couldn't see anything except cliffs when we were coming down in the plane. But obviously the boat has to be close by, so we'll have to look around for it."

"What if we can't find it?"

"You've got to have faith—to trust. Because when you do you'll act accordingly, and the Lord will help us. On the other hand, if we get discouraged we might not do anything right."

"I don't know," Tank said doubtfully.

"It's our responsibility to trust," Josh assured his friend, "and do what we can. If we don't locate the boat, we'll find another way to save ourselves."

Tank started to shake his head just as Tanner stopped ahead and called, "Pua, Keoni! Come here."

A boy about ten years old slid down from a giant banyan tree.* He dropped barefooted to the jungle floor. A girl of about 12 stepped out from behind the thick trunk of the same tree.

Josh sucked in his breath sharply and stepped back. Instead of a flower lei* around her neck, which would not have been unusual, a heavy-bodied snake about four feet long was draped there.

Tank, standing beside Josh, whispered hoarsely, "There are no snakes in Hawaii!"

"Well, there's one now!" Josh whispered back.

Tanner said, "Boys, this is the lieutenant's daughter, Pua, and her brother, Keoni. Kids, this dark-haired guy is Josh Ladd. The blond one is Tank Catlett. They're going to be staying with us, so all of you get acquainted. I'm going back to camp."

As he turned around, Josh shifted his gaze away from the huge snake to study the boy and girl before him. Both had golden-brown skin that revealed they were part Hawaiian and part Caucasian, or hapahaole.*

Their eyes were brown like their long hair. The boy wore only a pair of old swimming trunks. The girl, bareheaded and barefooted, wore a pair of blue jeans and an orchid-colored blouse.

Josh managed to smile and say, "Hi," which Tank echoed, also smiling.

Pua replied, "Hi," but she did not smile.

Keoni, her brother, asked, "You want to hold our snake?"

Josh and Tank vigorously shook their heads.

Josh felt his eyes unwillingly drawn back to the reptile, which glistened with shiny colors.

"It's a boa constrictor," the boy explained, taking it from his sister's neck and settling it about his own. "They grow to about ten feet, but this is a little one."

Tank muttered under his breath, "Looks plenty big to me."

Josh said, "I didn't think there were any snakes in Hawaii—well, except those brown tree snakes from Guam that they've started finding around the docks in Oahu.* So where did this one come from?"

"Daddy bought it from a ship," Keoni answered. "Same

with the other animals and birds back at camp."

"What's he going to do with them?" Tank asked.

"Sell them to the black market in Honolulu."

"Keoni!" His sister whirled to snap at him.

"Well, he will."

Josh glanced at Tank to see if he realized what Josh had just learned. *These men are smugglers as well as marijuana growers. They deal in illegal birds, snakes, and things like that.*

Pua broke into Josh's thoughts by changing the subject. "How'd you two get here?"

Josh and Tank explained.

Tank concluded, "I have to get back to camp and see how my dad's doing."

"After that," Keoni said as they started down the trail, "do you want to go swimming, or ti-leaf* sliding?"

Josh shook his head. "We just want to get home. But your father says we can't leave here—ever." He shoved a thick hanging vine from an overhead tree out of his way. "What do you think he's going to do to us?"

"I don't know. Nobody else has ever been here since we came."

Her brother said cheerfully, "That's okay. "Me 'n' Pua also plan to stay here always, so now I'll have somebody else to play with. Pua's no fun anymore. Mostly, she sits around and cries."

"Keoni!" his older sister said sharply.

"Well, it's true, so why're you yelling at me?" He turned to Josh and Tank. "You know what I like best about being here? We won't ever have to go back to school again! I hate school! Daddy says he's got enough books and things so we can learn right here."

Moving along the trail toward camp, Josh sought to learn as much about this strange group of people as possible. It might help him to understand more about how dangerous it was for himself, Tank, and Tank's father.

"How long have you lived here?" he asked.

"A couple of months," Pua replied. "Daddy came to Honolulu and got us after Mom died."

Josh said sincerely, "I'm sorry."

The girl looked at Josh with sad, brown eyes. "I wish..." she began, then hesitated.

"Wish what?"

"Never mind."

Josh frowned, wondering what she had been about to say. He saw the pain in her eyes, now suddenly bright with forming tears.

Josh turned to Keoni. "Did your father stay here in the jungle when you two lived in the city?"

"Before Mom died, she told us that he'd lived here for years." Keoni adjusted the snake around his neck. "Dad came out of the jungle when he finally heard about her being dead. We were living with our tutu.* I'm still mad at Mom for dying...."

"Keoni! Stop it!" his sister snapped, whirling to face him.

"I am mad at her! Why get huhu* because I said so?"

"It wasn't her fault, and you know it!" Pua's voice shot up. "I don't ever want to hear you say that again!"

"You don't have to bite my head off," Keoni muttered. He looked up at Josh and Tank to add, "She's mad all the time since Mom died, mostly at me."

Pua opened her mouth, then took a deep breath and slowly let it out. "He's too young to really understand," she explained sadly to Josh and Tank.

Josh nodded and asked, "How did she die?"

"Auto accident," Pua replied, her voice threatening to crack with emotion. She started running down the jungle trail. "Come on, let's get back to camp!"

When they reentered the clearing and walked by the cages, the birds uttered hoarse cries and flew about. The cats in their kennels mewed loudly and stuck their paws through the wire mesh.

Josh didn't hear the dog barking and looked into its kennel. The door stood open. The kennel was empty.

"Where's the dog?" Josh asked.

"Over there," Keoni pointed.

Josh saw the skinny animal standing by a water bowl but not drinking. The dog studied the boys with baleful eyes.

"What's his name?" Josh asked.

"Maka. It means 'eyes' in Hawaiian," Keoni said. "His eyes are really strange. You want to see up close?"

"Maybe later." Josh started to look away just as the dog staggered. "What's wrong with him?" he asked.

"I don't know," Keoni explained. "He hasn't acted just right the last few days."

A cold chill swept over Josh's body. "How long have you had him?" he asked with forced casualness.

"Oh, a few weeks or so."

"Where'd you get him?"

"Off the same ship where my dad got the cats, the birds, and the snake," Keoni replied. "It came from Asia."

"So none of them have been through the quarantine at Honolulu?"

"No. Why?" Keoni cocked his head and looked suspiciously at Josh.

"Oh, nothing. I was just thinking." Josh walked a few steps, then asked casually, "You mentioned that your father has a lot of books. Does he have a set of encyclopedias?"

"Sure does. Want to borrow one?" Keoni replied.

"Do you think your father would mind if I did?"

"He won't care. He lets Pua and me use them. Which one do you want? I'll get it for you."

"How about the one that includes R?"

"R for what?" Keoni asked.

Josh answered evasively. "Just borrow the one where the R's start, please."

"Be right back," Keoni said, turning away. "But first I've got to put the snake back in his cage."

"Good riddance!" Tank muttered with relief. Then he asked, "Josh, What do you want to look up that begins with an R?"

"Rabies." He said the dread word softly.

"Rabies?" Tank scoffed. "There's never been a case of rabies in the islands, because there's such a strict quarantine about incoming animals."

"I know, but these animals haven't been quarantined. Something I read a long time ago about the symptoms of rabies makes me worried now."

"Oh, great!" Tank grumbled. "That's all we need on top of our other problems."

"I could be wrong," Josh admitted, but inwardly he felt a new and terrible fear.

Tank led the way to where his father was propped up on a folding army cot in front of one of the four tents. Tank asked anxiously, "How do you feel, Dad?"

"Still have a monstrous headache, and my leg hurts, but I'll be okay." He asked, "Who's your new friend?"

"Keoni, the lieutenant's son." Tank pointed to where the girl was talking with her father and the sergeant. "That's his sister. Her name's Pua."

Sam Catlett nodded and lowered his voice so only the two boys standing beside him could hear. "I tried again to talk Beacher into letting us go, but he became so upset I shut up for fear he'd do us some harm."

"Josh and I've been planning how to escape," Tank

whispered. "We know they have a boat, but we don't know where."

"I've been thinking along those lines too," Sam Catlett said. "It's not logical that those two men would let us stay here indefinitely—eating their food, sleeping in their tents, all that sort of thing.

"Besides, sooner or later, we'll get on each others' nerves. Beacher is obviously mentally unstable, so if he becomes angry enough at us, he could do something violent."

Josh said fervently, "We have to find a way to escape! And soon!"

"If we could just find their boat!" Tank mused.

"Or send a message to the Coast Guard!" Josh added.

Keoni came running back with a thick encyclopedia volume. "Here's the one you wanted, Josh."

"Thanks." He took the volume with a silent prayer, *Lord, I hope I'm wrong! But I have to be sure! If he has rabies...*

The fearful thought caused gooseflesh to suddenly appear on Josh's arms as he opened the encyclopedia.

Chapter Four

THE LEGEND OF CAPTAIN KIDD

Tank's father asked, "What are you looking up?"
Josh squatted down to put the heavy encyclopedia on the ground. He flipped through the pages. "Rabies."

Mr. Catlett asked sharply, "Why are you interested in that topic?"

Josh hesitated, unwilling to scare the others when there was no clear evidence. "Uh...I wanted to check some symptoms." He ran his finger down the page.

"Symptoms for what?" Tank's father asked.

"Rabies." Josh barely whispered the word.

Keoni asked, "What's rabies?"

Josh avoided the boy's eyes. "A disease."

Keoni asked, "You think that's what Maka has?"

Josh shrugged. "I don't know. The book says that it's almost impossible to tell if an animal has rabies simply by looking."

Mr. Catlett asked, "So what did you see that made you look up the subject, Josh?"

"I saw Maka stagger, and it says here that sometimes an infected animal does that." Josh squinted at the dog. "And he's got a vacant stare, but it says that is not a positive sign either." Josh looked back at Keoni. "Have you seen Maka drink lately?"

"No, but he's been standing there by the water bowl for a long time. Why?"

"Another word for rabies is hydrophobia, meaning 'fear of water.' But the book says that's not true. A rabid animal may want to drink, but can't because it can't close its jaws just right."

"But if Maka has rabies, can he bite?" Keoni asked with obvious concern.

"Oh, yes! He could bite us, the cats, or any other warm-blooded animals, wild or domestic." Josh stood up and handed the encyclopedia to Keoni. "Thanks for bringing me this."

The little boy's eyes were wide with fright. "Will I die if Maka has rabies and bites me?"

Josh answered carefully but truthfully. "Not if a doctor gives you some special shots."

"There's no doctor around here, and Dad hates leaving the bush." Fear drove Keoni's voice up. He gulped, then added, "Maybe there are no shots like that anywhere in the islands, because there's never been a case of rabies here. We learned that in school."

Josh tried to sound reassuring. "It's probably all right, but

I'd stay away from the dog if I were you. I'll tell your father and Mr. Tanner, just in case." Josh turned to where the men were talking with Pua.

"I'll go with you," Keoni said.

"So will I," Tank decided.

"Let's all go," Mr. Catlett added. He got to his feet, then winced in pain and sat down again on the cot.

"You okay?" Josh asked.

"That leg hurts when I put weight on it, and I felt a little dizzy," Mr. Catlett answered. "Maybe you boys had better go ahead, and I'll rest some more."

Josh and Tank exchanged concerned glances as they headed toward the two men. They were talking with Pua at the outdoor table.

Keoni ran ahead, holding up the heavy encyclopedia volume. "Josh thinks Maka's got rabies!"

Beacher and Tanner turned to face Josh and Tank as the boys stood across the table from them.

"What's this?" the lieutenant asked bruskly.

Josh briefly explained his suspicions about the dog and pointed out the encyclopedia article. He concluded, "I could be wrong, but I thought I'd better tell you."

Beacher shook his head. "I don't think you're right, Josh, but I obviously can't take any risks with my children. Sergeant, cage the dog away from the other animals, just to be sure."

"Be careful," Josh urged as the man with the rifle turned

to obey.

"I've neglected my manners," Beacher commented to Josh and Tank. "You boys must be hungry."

Josh honestly hadn't thought about it, but he became aware of how sticky his skin was from where the saltwater had dried. "We could eat," he agreed. "But I'd rather wash up...."

He broke off, suddenly thinking of a way to get back to the beach where they might find the hidden boat or be seen by searchers. "Maybe we could go swimming."

Keoni spoke up quickly. "How about the Toilet Bowl? That's fun, huh, Pua?"

As the girl nodded, Josh asked, "What's that?"

Keoni started to explain, "It's from an underground lava tube...." He stopped talking as the heavy beat of a low-flying helicopter sounded overhead.

Everyone looked up.

Beach commented, "They're probably looking for you survivors. But they'll never see you under these trees."

Josh and Tank glanced helplessly at each other.

"Awhile ago," the lieutenant continued, "I was at the lava tube opening by the beach where you washed ashore. I saw a couple of fixed-wing aircraft flying low over the water. There were also a few boats, but they didn't come in close. Their skippers all know how treacherous the coral reefs are around here."

He turned to his daughter. "Pua, would you warm up

some rice for our guests? Keoni, you can see if there's some dried squid for them."

Josh suppressed an inward groan. He had never gotten used to the Hawaiian way of serving rice instead of potatoes at almost every meal. He certainly didn't like squid, an island delicacy. *It's like chewing on rubber bands,* he thought. But he mumbled his thanks.

Josh and Tank started to follow the lieutenant's children as they headed toward the cooking area. But Beacher suggested, "Josh, you and Tank may as well relax. Tell me about yourselves."

Josh glanced up, trying to see through the dense canopy overhead. It was so thick that he glimpsed only a flash of the chopper before it turned out to sea. His spirits sagged, knowing there was no way an aerial search would ever see the hidden camp. He and his friends would have to find some way to be on the beach if searchers were to see them.

Josh and Tank sat on the homemade benches across the table from the bush vet. "Not much to tell," Josh said. "We'd much rather hear about you, wouldn't we, Tank?"

Tank nodded and asked, "Did you and Sergeant Tanner serve a long time together in Vietnam?"

A cloud seemed to drift across the man's eyes. His jaw muscles twitched as if some bitter memories were flickering through his mind.

"You boys do any diving?" he asked abruptly, changing the subject.

"Mostly free diving with snorkels," Josh replied.

"We also scuba dive sometimes," Tank added.

Josh remembered seeing the shipwrecks under the clear Pacific waters as the plane was coming down. "How about you, Mister...uh...Lieutenant Beacher? You ever dive on those wrecks off that beach where you found us?"

The man chuckled. "I like to dive, but I'm no fool. Those wrecks are protected by some of the most dangerous currents in the islands. There were rumors about old pirate's ships being sunk there. Divers who thought they'd find gold or jewels or other treasure have tried to explore those wrecks, but they all lost their lives. Now nobody in his right mind comes near them anymore."

The lieutenant leaned forward, placing his elbows on the table and cupping his chin in his palms. "You boys ever play pirate?" he asked.

When they both nodded, the man continued. "Pirates are fascinating. For centuries, piracy was common around the world. Naturally, masters of pirate ships operating in the Pacific Ocean had to come ashore for fresh water, provisions, and so forth. Hawaii was such a place.

"So a legend grew up that this remote section of the Big Island is where pirates sometimes landed. But the reefs and currents are so treacherous that the few ships that tried to investigate ended up on the bottom."

Josh asked, "How did you find this place without getting sunk?"

"I came overland. I'd been living in the bush for a long time. One day, by accident, I stumbled upon this place."

Josh's mind leaped at the possibility that there was another way of escape besides by boat.

Beacher added, "But you boys will never find it. You'd get lost in the jungle and die there. So don't even think about it."

Josh felt his hopes sag, realizing the lieutenant was right about getting lost. Then Josh thought of something else. "You have supplies that are too big to carry, like hundred-pound bags of rice, and all those sacks and cans of feed for the birds and animals."

He pointed to where Keoni was scooping out the white grains for a pan his sister held. "Since you don't have any horses or other animals big enough to carry things like that, you have to bring them in either by boat or helicopter. I don't see any place where a chopper could land, so it must be by boat."

"Yeah," Tank added. "We saw Mr. Tanner in a boat when we were coming down. But he disappeared."

Beacher smiled. "You're both pretty smart kids. Now you know we also have a boat. But if you're thinking of escaping that way, forget it. You'll never find where it's hidden."

Josh suppressed a sigh of disappointment. He avoided looking at Tank, knowing he was also silently hurting over the bad news.

The lieutenant asked, "You boys read about pirates back when you played at being them?"

Josh volunteered, "My father was a history teacher on the Mainland, so I learned some things from him."

"Such as?" the lieutenant prompted.

"Well, I remember some pirates' names, like Jean Lafitte."*

"Actually," the lieutenant said, "Lafitte was a French privateer, not a pirate. He operated privately owned ships with his government's permission to attack Spanish shipping off the Texas and Louisiana coasts. On the other hand, a pirate acted on his own, without authorization, robbing for personal profit on the seas."

Josh admitted, "I didn't know that." He added, "Bully Hayes was one of the last pirates to work out of San Francisco. He might have landed here in Hawaii. Then there was Blackbeard, whose real name was Edward Teach."

"What do you know about Captain Kidd?"

Josh hesitated, instantly wary. "Uh...my father said there's some question about him."

"What kind of question?"

Josh squirmed uncomfortably, unable to understand why the man before him had earlier pretended to be Kidd. Josh also feared that a wrong answer could cause the lieutenant to erupt into one of his violent moods.

"Well, Dad said there's some doubt about whether he was a real historical character or not," Josh explained. "He was sort of legendary."

Beacher smiled and closed his eyes. "A legend. I like

that." He opened his eyes again and smiled. "Maybe we can have some good conversations in days to come."

With sudden determination, Josh looked the man straight in the eye. "Look, Lieutenant, we have to get home! If you'll let us go down to the beach, we can signal a passing plane or boat. We'll promise not to say anything about you—ever."

"You don't understand, Josh," the man said firmly. "You see, years ago, I went into the bush to live the way I want, away from the pressures of civilized life. Then I had to bring my children here, and that's a problem.

"But you three coming has given me worse problems. On the one hand, I want you gone, but on the other hand, I can't let you go. So, until I figure out what to do, you three must absolutely not go near that beach."

His tone softened slightly as he explained, "You're too much of a risk. By now, you've figured out why I have all those exotic animals. Maybe you even stumbled over some of my pokololo plants."

He paused, shook his head, and continued. "No, you didn't, or you'd be full of punji stick holes."

Josh's flesh crawled at the possibility of stumbling into some of the booby traps.* At the same time, Josh's anxiety made him angry. "You can't keep us here forever!" he flared, frustration getting the better of him. "My parents and Tank's mom will never stop searching for us! They'll find us, and when they do..."

Suddenly Beacher jumped up from the table, eyes

blazing. "Be ye threatening mutiny?" he demanded angrily. His personality totally changed in an instant. "Mr. Hook!" the captain roared, "Prepare the plank!"

Josh backed up rapidly as the red-bearded man stalked deliberately around the table toward him, his bald scalp a dark red from the blood surging angrily through his head.

"I'm sorry!" Josh exclaimed. "I didn't mean . . ."

"Daddy, please!" Pua rushed up to block her father's way. "Daddy, stop!"

As the lieutenant stared down at the girl, Josh heard the sergeant run up. He called in a hoarse whisper, "Boys, stand still and shut up! He'll get over it in a minute."

Josh obeyed, his heart flopping wildly against his ribs, but his eyes stayed on Beacher.

Slowly, the fury faded from his face. He relaxed slightly, looking down at his daughter. "What's the matter, Pua?" he asked in apparent bewilderment.

She exclaimed, "Oh, Daddy!" and threw her arms around him, burying her face against his chest. "You scared me again!"

"Scared *her*?" Tank croaked from beside Josh.

"Shh!" Josh hissed.

For a long moment, nobody moved or said anything. Then Beacher kissed Pua on top of her head and gently freed himself from her arms. Wordlessly, he left everyone standing and hurried toward his tent.

"What's he going to do?" Josh asked Pua.

She replied quietly, "He's gone after his gun."

Chapter Five

THE
TOILET BOWL

Josh gulped hard, vainly trying to swallow the lump of fear that had suddenly formed in his throat. "Getting his gun?" Josh croaked.

Pua said soothingly, "It's all right. He'll go into the bush and fire off a few rounds."

Tanner added, "He does that sometimes. Then he'll be okay again."

Josh took a long, shuddering breath and slowly let it out. "Oh!" he said.

Josh and Tank hurried to explain to Mr. Catlett, who had witnessed the whole event.

Almost immediately, the lieutenant emerged from his tent with a duplicate of the automatic weapon Tanner carried. He disappeared into the jungle. Moments later, the sound of many rounds being fired could be heard.

Josh was still a little apprehensive and tense when the firing died away and the lieutenant returned from the bush with the weapon.

43

Beacher looked at everyone and smiled. "Thought I saw some wild pigs," he explained. He carried the rifle to his tent and disappeared inside.

Standing with Tank and Keoni by the cooking fire where Pua was preparing rice, Josh spoke with feeling. "Thanks, Pua! If you hadn't stepped in, I might have been badly hurt." He hesitated, then continued, "If I can do anything for you, let me know."

Pua looked at him with sad brown eyes. "There's only one thing I want..." Her sentence trailed off.

"What is it?" Josh prompted.

Pua shook her head so her long dark hair swayed gently across her shoulders. "You can't help. Nobody can."

"Try me."

She considered Josh's earnest face, then looked at her little brother. "Keoni and I want our daddy to be well again."

"But we don't know how," the boy added.

Josh thought quickly. "Your father's a veteran, and there's an army hospital at Honolulu. They have doctors who could..."

"No!" Pua interrupted firmly. "No doctors! They might keep him there, and he'd die! Mom said that when he came back from the war, he tried to live in Honolulu. But he couldn't stand it, so he took off for the bush. Mom said there was something about the jungles that drew him back."

She shivered slightly. "Mom told us that it's caused by the terrible memories he has of things that happened in Vietnam.

He wouldn't even tell Mom about them."

Keoni spoke up. "She used to say that she didn't worry too much, because the sergeant was with him, just like they were in Vietnam. But Mom missed Daddy a lot. She cried when she didn't think Pua or I heard her."

"But the only way he's likely to get well," Josh protested, "is if he has some doctors to help him, doctors who understand such things."

Pua sighed. "Keoni and I have talked about that. But we can't take a chance that anyone would take away his freedom, even if we could talk Daddy into going to see a doctor."

"Some day he might hurt somebody," Josh warned. "I mean, the way he switches back and forth from being gentle and nice to yelling and threatening violence."

"He's all right unless somebody upsets him," Pua protested. "Then these spells—that's what Mom used to call them—pass. You've seen that happen."

"But suppose you or your brother upset him..." Josh began.

Pua again interrupted. "No doctors, I said! Now, please leave me alone!"

As Josh and Tank reluctantly walked away, Keoni fell into step beside them. "She's going to cry again, and she didn't want you guys to see. But she'll be okay after awhile. Then we can all go to the Toilet Bowl."

"What's that?" Tank asked.

"You'll see," Keoni said with a teasing smile. "Come on,

I'll show you around while Pua's finishing your food."

The colorful and exotic birds set up a chorus of harsh and discordant cries as the three boys approached the cages at the far end of the open area. The cats joined in with plaintive mewing, but Maka, the dog, stared silently with head lowered.

"He makes me nervous," Tank muttered as they passed his cage. "Keoni, how strong is that wire? Could he get out if he tried real hard?"

The boy shook his head. "Daddy doesn't want any of these birds or animals to escape into the jungle. He and Sergeant Tanner used the strongest wire they could buy. See how it goes across the top so nothing can get out that way?"

When Josh and Tank nodded, Keoni continued. "The wire on the sides is also buried two feet underground. That's not only to keep the dog or cats from digging out,but to keep mongooses* from digging in. They'd kill all the birds, you know."

"How'd they get all this stuff in here?" Josh asked. "I mean, the wire, the posts, the gates, the hinges, and all that?"

"It was here when Pua and I came to live with Dad. But the sergeant once told me that a ship brought it. Of course, it couldn't come in close because of the reefs, so he and Dad took our boat out to the ship and brought things in that way."

Josh tried to keep his voice casual. "Where do they keep the boat?"

Keoni shook his head. "Dad would get mad at me if I told

you."

Tank asked, "Then how about the ship? When does it come?"

"No regular time." Keoni pointed to the last cage in the row. "There goes a mongoose! See? He was probably trying to find a way into that bird cage."

Josh caught a flash of brown as the slender, two-foot-long carnivore disappeared into the underbrush.

Pua called, so the three boys turned back toward the center of camp. As they walked side by side, Keoni asked, "Are you planning to escape?"

Josh looked down at the ten-year-old. "What makes you ask that?" he asked evasively.

"Because if I was kept someplace where I couldn't ever see my family, I'd try to go home."

"We want to go home, of course," Josh replied. "But when I said something about that to your father a while ago, you saw how angry he was with me."

"When are you going to try?" Keoni wanted to know.

Josh looked at Tank, then shrugged. "I don't think we should talk about it, because your father might be upset with you."

"I guess you're right. But if you are rescued or escape, would you tell the police or anybody about Daddy?"

Josh frowned. "Do you want us to do that?"

"If that could help our daddy get well, yes. Otherwise, no. I like it here, but Pua doesn't."

Keoni paused, looking toward the tent where Mr. Catlett rested on the army cot. "Even if you two could get away, he can't go. Not on that bum leg. So what'll you do with him?"

Neither Josh nor Tank replied, but the question nagged Josh during the meal of rice that Pua had prepared. The question still rang through Josh's mind after lunch when he and Tank told Mr. Catlett they were going to swim with Pua and Keoni.

"Not for fun," Josh whispered. "We're hoping to find where the boat is hidden. Or maybe we'll see a ship or plane and can signal them so they'll know where we are."

Tank's father cautioned, "Be careful, boys. Mr. Beacher is a very strange man. I don't like his sudden fits of violence."

"We'll be careful," Tank replied.

As the boys started across the open area to where Pua and Keoni waited, Tank said, "Dad doesn't look very well to me. Did you notice?"

Josh nodded. "He was rather quiet, but maybe that's because he still has a headache from when he banged his head as the plane hit the water."

"Well, at least he seems to be none the worse for not breathing for a minute or so after nearly drowning. But I'm more worried about that coral cut. Suppose it becomes infected?"

"That's another reason why we either have to be rescued or escape and bring back some medical help."

Tank said doubtfully, "That might not be easy. What if

those men start shooting at whoever comes to help us?"

"We'll just have to do what we can, and pray."

Josh's hope rose slightly when he saw that Pua and Keoni led the way through a narrow passage in the mountain. It opened onto a narrow, black lava shelf. The Pacific Ocean spread majestically before them, but there was no sign of a boat, plane, or helicopter.

"Watch your step," Pua warned as she and her brother picked their way along the foot-wide ledge. About 50 yards from the ocean she stopped. "Here's the Toilet Bowl," she explained.

"Isn't it neat?" her brother asked. "Look!"

Josh and Tank joined them in looking down at a kind of large hole or pit in the ancient lava. He guessed the hole was about 12 feet across and maybe 15 feet deep. It was empty except for about a foot of foaming water at the bottom. There was a kind of sucking sound like water draining out of a massive bathtub.

Tank guessed, "This must be what a blowhole is like, except with a tiny opening instead of a wide one."

Josh nodded, remembering the spouting holes he'd seen on Oahu and Kauai.* His eyes followed the last of the water where it drained out a large hole at the bottom of the Toilet Bowl. The opening was about as wide as Josh's hips, but smaller than his shoulders.

Pua explained, "There's an underground lava tube running from the ocean to this place. As the waves come toward the shore, water rushes through that tube and fills up this pit."

"And that's also where the water drains out," her brother added. "When the waves on the shore and the water runs back into the ocean, the water in this pit drains out through the tube. There's one like it at Hanauma Bay* near Koko Head* outside of Honolulu. You guys ever see that one?"

"We've snorkeled in that bay," Josh said, "but I've never seen anything like this."

"Me either," Tank added.

"It's around the side of the bay," Keoni said, "so not everybody knows it's there. Oh, the water's starting to come in! Get your shoes off! We'll show you one of the most fun rides you've ever had!"

In 30 to 40 seconds, the incoming flow of sea water had filled the pit to the top. Pua and her brother jumped in fully clothed.

"Come on!" Pua cried, motioning for Josh and Tank to join her and her brother. "When the water drains out, it'll feel like going down in one of those Honolulu elevators, only faster."

Josh hesitated, looking dubiously at the strange pit. "Why not?" he said, and quickly removed his heavy hiking boots.

Tank did the same.

Barefooted, but fully clothed, the two friends jumped feet first into the pit. They sank beneath the surface, then quickly popped to the top. The water had stopped running and was steady.

"Ready?" Pua asked. "It's about to start down."

Josh was surprised at how fast the water drained out through the lava tube, dropping him rapidly along with his three companions. Josh glanced in some alarm at Pua and Keoni. They didn't seem at all concerned.

Josh glanced away from the rapidly dropping water in the pit to look with some anxiety at the top, where they had stood on solid lava moments before. The rim seemed to rush upward, away from them. He felt better when his feet touched the rough bottom, but the rapid outgoing suction was so strong that he had to brace his feet against the powerful tug.

I'd sure hate to get sucked into that tube! he thought as the water fell silent. Only a few inches of water remained on the bottom of the pit. Then it was strangely quiet.

"Wasn't that fun?" Pua's voice echoed strangely, as if she was in the bottom of a shallow well.

"I'll say!" Tank exclaimed.

Josh didn't say anything. He glanced apprehensively at the top of the pit far above. Only a patch of blue sky with one puffy white cloud showed. Josh felt the experience had been more scary that he wanted to admit, especially in front of Pua, but he managed to smile at her and her brother.

Keoni explained, "The water will come back in about 30 or 40 seconds, just like the waves do on the shore."

Josh looked up at the top of the hole, frowning at how far away it seemed. *But it's only about 15 feet,* he reminded himself. Still, he wondered how anyone would ever get out if the water didn't return.

"Wait'll you start up!" Keoni said. "You'll think you're going to shoot right up into the sky! Listen, I can hear it starting to come back through the tube."

Almost instantly, a foot-wide stream of water spurted from the tube. It shot far out into the pit, striking Josh's legs so hard he staggered slightly. He was surprised at how fast the water filled the bottom of the pit. One moment, only his ankles were covered. Then the water passed his knees and reached his chest.

Pua shouted. "Here we go!"

The power of the incoming water lifted everyone upward like a fighter jet lifting off a runway.

Above the noise of the inrushing water, Josh heard a familiar beating in the air. "Tank, listen!"

"Helicopter!" Tank cried, looking upward. "They're looking for us!"

A big helicopter with a bright orange stripe flew into view at the right side of the pit.

"Coast Guard!" Josh exclaimed. He started waving and shouting. "Hey, look down here!"

"We're too far down in this pit," Tank groaned. "They'll never see us."

"We've got to try!" Josh shouted. "As soon as we reach the top, jump out. Wave and shout!"

The pit that had started filling with scary rapidity started slowing. In desperation, Josh reached high over his head and gripped the top of the pit as the rising water almost stopped.

"Here we are!" he shouted, desperately clawing to scramble out over the top of the rim. *O Lord, make them see us!*

When he threw himself out of the water and leaped to his feet, the helicopter was directly overhead.

"Down here!" Josh yelled mightily, waving his arms and jumping up and down. "We're here. Look down here!"

Chapter Six

ANCIENT HAWAIIAN LEGENDS

Ignoring the uneven black lava under his bare feet, Josh ran along the path by the Toilet Bowl, wildly waving both arms over his head.

"Down here!" Josh screamed toward the Coast Guard helicopter as it flew low, moving rapidly from directly overhead toward the left. "We're down here!"

Josh was aware that Tank was also shouting and waving, frantically trying to attract the attention of the chopper crew. Out of the corner of his eye, Josh saw Pua and Keoni climb from the pit as the water started draining.

"Look this way!" Josh shouted toward the helicopter. His throat hurt from yelling so hard. "Look down! Oh, please see us!"

The aircraft moved steadily past and out of sight.

Stunned with this crushing failure, Josh sank weakly onto the rough lava by the Toilet Bowl. With aching heart he stared at the silent sky. *Now what?*

Pua's voice roused him from his anguish. "I shouldn't say

anything, but—I'm sorry."

"Thanks."

Keoni said, "Dad would really be mad if the Coast Guard had seen you guys, though."

His sister agreed. "That's right, so we'd better not come here anymore, or go anywhere along the shore."

Josh looked in dismay at Tank, who silently mouthed something. The beach—Josh was sure that's what Tank meant. Josh nodded briefly. *There goes our chance to get down where we landed and try to leave an S.O.S. on the sand,* he told himself. *Well, now we'll have to find that boat. It's our only other way out of this place.*

As they headed back in silent dejection, Pua reached out and gently touched Josh's forearm. "Did you mean what you said earlier about helping Dad?"

"Of course. You probably saved my life back there in camp awhile ago."

"I don't think Daddy would really hurt anyone, but sometimes I'm not sure. Keoni and I have talked about it, and, well, we're sort of worried."

"She means we're scared of Daddy having one of his spells and getting mad at us, or even his friend."

"Or maybe the sergeant will get upset with Daddy and hurt him," Pua added.

Josh said, "I thought they got along real well?"

"They do, most of the time. But sometimes when Dad thinks he's Captain Kidd, he gets angry at the sergeant," Pua explained. "Then Daddy thinks he's his first mate, and calls him Mr. Hook. So far, the sergeant has managed to keep out of Daddy's way until the spell passes."

"But the sergeant has a temper too," Keoni said.

"He has?" Josh asked in surprise.

"A terrible one," Keoni assured Josh. "I saw him kick Maka once, so I sure wouldn't want to make him mad."

Josh looked at Tank to see if he was having the same growing uneasiness that gnawed at Josh's insides. He saw Tank gulp, and guessed that meant he was feeling the same thing.

"If we could get back to Honolulu," Josh said carefully, trying to plant a seed thought in Pua's mind, "my father could see that both these men find help. Dad owns a tourist publication, so he knows lots of important people all over these islands."

Pua shot a glance at her brother, then said, "I have to talk to Keoni. You two go on ahead. But when you come to the top of that next hill, stop and wait for us."

Puzzled, Josh and Tank went on, discussing what the brother and sister were talking about.

"Maybe they're going to help us," Josh concluded as he puffed up to the top of the hill and sat down to wait.

Tank sank beside him. "That'd sure be nice."

Josh let his eyes roam down the other side of the hill. "This isn't the way we came," he observed. "We didn't see those kukui trees* in that wet gulch on our way to the ocean."

Their light green leaves made them easy to recognize from a distance.

Tank suddenly stiffened. "Hey, there's water down at the bottom of that draw! See its reflection?"

Josh followed his friend's pointing hand. "I see it. It's too wide to be a stream." He stood up quickly. "That must be a little cove or inlet from the ocean. Hey, you know what?"

"Yeah, the boat!" Tank exclaimed, jumping up. "I'll bet that's where the boat is hidden!"

"And Pua must have deliberately let us come up here alone so we could figure that out."

"Too bad we can't go down there right now and make sure." Tank's usual slow, soft voice rose in excitement. "But Pua and Keoni are starting up this way. We'll have to come back by ourselves, maybe tonight after everyone else is asleep."

"Let's make sure we remember the way. Boy, we'll have to find out if the boat has plenty of gasoline, and if it needs a key to start the motor."

"Maybe it has a rope starter, like a lawn mower."

"Even so, it'll have a key. The question is, do they leave the key in the ignition, or take it with them?"

Tank groaned. "If they take it, then who has it—the lieutenant or the sergeant?"

"We'll have to find out," Josh replied, then fell silent as Pua and Keoni approached.

Keoni asked, "Is your skin as sticky as mine?"

"Sure is," Josh admitted. "The trade winds dry the saltwater real fast and make my skin feel terrible."

"Maybe you'd like to go swimming in fresh water and wash the salt off," Pua suggested. "There's a waterfall and a pool near here."

Josh wanted to get back to camp and tell Tank's father about finding where the boat might be hidden. But that news could wait. "Suits me," Josh said. "Tank?"

"Sounds good to me."

"Then we'll go this way," Pua said. She turned toward the mountain range at the back of the pocket valley. "It's not far."

Keoni fell into step with his sister but looked over his shoulder to Josh and Tank. "Maybe the mo'o* won't let us swim, but if he does, then we can go ti-leaf sliding at the same time."

"Tank and I've gone ti-leaf sliding," Josh said, following a couple of steps behind Pua and Keoni. "But what's a mo'o?"

"That means 'lizard,'" Keoni replied. "Up ahead, when we come out from under the trees, you'll see a mountain that looks like a lizard. He's the guardian of the pool where we're going to swim—that is, if the ti leaf floats."

Josh and Tank looked at each other. Both shrugged.

Josh asked, "What do you mean, 'if the leaf floats'?"

"We have to find out if the mo'o will let us swim, so we put a ti-leaf on the water. If it floats, that means it's okay to swim. If it sinks, we can't go in, because that would make the mo'o angry, and something terrible could happen. Like he could pull us down."

"It's supposed to be a bottomless pool," Pua added.

Josh said, "I know about some Hawaiian superstitions, but..."

"Superstitions?" Pua repeated, turning around and stopping in the trail. "Are you making fun of what we believe?"

"No," Josh replied hastily. "I guess I used the wrong word. I'm interested in Hawaiian legends and beliefs."

When the girl's eyes remained suspicious, Josh quickly added, "Tank and I know about the local belief in Pele, goddess of the volcanoes. But I'd never heard of this mo'o and the floating ti leaf."

Pua seemed satisfied. "Tell them, Keoni," she said, and again started walking.

"Well," the boy continued, striding beside his sister, "our tutu told us that the mo'o originally came from the ocean, where it fought with a shark. Then mo'o returned to the mountain, where it died. Mo'o's body is in the mountain, but his spirit lies in the bottomless pool where we're going."

"So," Pua concluded, "let's hurry and find out whether we can swim today."

She soon led them out of the rain forest into an open area of lush green vegetation and brilliant flowering plants and trees.

Keoni pointed out the mountain formation that resembled a giant lizard at the end of the valley. There was a 200-foot cliff below the reptile's head. A waterfall seemed to originate from unseen cracks at the top of the volcanic mountain. After a freefall straight down the cliff, the water splattered against a flat area of polished lava, then cascaded over a final 20-foot falls to end in a large blue pool. Clumps of ti plants grew on both sides of it.

For a moment, Josh stood in silent appreciation. The exotic beauty of the secluded spot temporarily removed his eagerness to escape from the men who held them captive.

"We have to swim across to the slide if the mo'o will let us," Pua explained, pointing.

Josh lifted his eyes past the waterfall to examine a long, narrow natural groove in the surface of the slanting mountain side. The channel was about three feet wide, a foot deep, and 30 yards long. It ended at the narrow end of the pool near where the waterfall completed its descent. A long vine stretched across the channel about two feet from its end and perhaps three feet above.

"What's that for?" Josh asked.

Keoni laughed. "See that clump of bamboo growing on the other side of the pool?"

"Yes."

"If you don't grab that vine and slow yourself down, you'll shoot across the pool and land in the bamboo instead of the water. Big owie!"

Josh flinched, recalling his experience in crawling through wild bamboo near his home in Hawaii. "I'll remember," he promised.

On Oahu,* the island where Josh and Tank lived, they usually had to carry water from a pool to wet down the groove when they wanted to go ti-leaf siding. However, this one was perpetually moist from the waterfall's drifting spray.

"Now," Keoni said, "Let's see if it's okay to swim." He walked to the common wild shrub that Polynesians had introduced to the Hawaiian Islands centuries ago. The ti plants ranged from about three to ten feet tall. Keoni selected one of the shiny, long, broad leaves and carried it to the pool side.

Josh, Tank, and Pua watched expectantly as Keoni gently set the leaf on the pool's surface.

"It floats!" he shouted. "Everybody in!" He dived into the water behind the bobbing ti leaf.

Pua followed him gracefully into the clear blue water.

For the moment Josh forgot his problems and removed his boots. Tank did the same. They plunged in together, surfaced, and swam across the pool after Pua and her brother.

"You guys want to go down the slide first?" Keoni asked, hoisting himself out on the far side of the pool just below where the waterfall splashed noisily.

"I think you should be first," Josh said, and Tank nodded agreement.

Keoni approached another ti plant and pulled off a leaf. Carrying it, he scrambled up a short, steep path between broad-leafed banana plants interspersed with red ginger blossoms to where the channel began. Holding on to the top of the grooved side with his right hand, he gently eased himself down into the slippery channel. With his left hand, he placed the leaf in the groove, then quickly seated himself on the leaf.

The leaf on the wet slide acted like grease, so that the moment Keoni let go of the sides, he shot down the groove at a dizzying speed. Seconds later, with a happy yell, he sailed out of the groove, grabbed the vine stretched there, sailed over the pool and landed with a mighty splash.

Pua was next. She was followed by Tank, who seemed to temporarily forget his problems as he zipped down the slide and splashed into the pool.

Josh, coming last, was surprised how fast he was sliding. He reached up to grab the restraining vine as he neared the end of the ride. He clutched the vine with his right hand, but missed with his left. His momentum threw him to the right side instead of straight ahead. He sailed awkwardly through the air.

"Oh, no!" he cried, fearing he was about to land in the bamboo clumps. At the last moment, he fell into the shallow water just short of the shore.

Everyone howled with laughter as Josh sheepishly looked up from his embarrassing near-disaster. Josh managed to smile, but he felt pretty silly. He determined to make sure he got both hands on the vine after this.

The water was surprisingly cold. It gave Josh gooseflesh and set his teeth to chattering. But he didn't want to disgrace himself by being the first to dry off, so he forced himself to continue sliding and swimming until Pua hoisted herself out on the green bank to stretch out in the sunshine.

Josh swam over. "Mind if I join you?"

"I guess not."

I guess she's not still mad at me for what I said about superstitions, Josh told himself. He and Tank weren't superstitious, but many islanders strongly believed in ancient lore. That included non-Hawaiians.

Josh brushed the water from his brown hair and felt the warm trade winds starting to dry his body. "Pua," he said, facing her, "I meant what I said earlier about helping you any way I can."

"I wish you could." She sighed softly. "I've been thinking about what you said," she continued, turning sad brown eyes on his blue ones.

Her lower lip began to tremble. "I'd like my daddy to get some help. Like from a doctor who knew about how people's minds work. Maybe one of those doctors at the hospital you mentioned in Honolulu. Are you sure they wouldn't hurt him?"

Josh explained, "I've never known anybody who went there, but I'm sure they wouldn't hurt him. After all, he's sick. Well, he's really wounded, not in the arm or leg or someplace in the body, but in his mind."

"I'm afraid that if he doesn't get help, someday he's going to do something awful. Then he'd be hunted down, no matter where he lives—even here." Pua took a slow, shuddering breath. "I don't think Keoni or I could stand it if something awful happened to our father."

"If he was in the hospital for awhile, do you have anyone to live with? Keoni mentioned your grandmother."

"She lives on the windward side of Oahu. We stayed with her after Mom died and before Daddy came and got us. We could live with her again."

Josh felt his hopes begin to stir again. He pointed out, "All that depends on Tank, his father, and me getting away from here very soon."

Pua abruptly changed the subject. "We'd better get back to camp," she said, calling her brother and Tank.

Josh's hopes sagged as he returned, but he remembered the probability that he and Tank had discovered the boat's location.

If we can get down here tonight and make sure... Josh started to tell himself, but broke off when he saw the sergeant hurrying toward them, rifle at the ready.

"Pua!" he called, "did you kids see the dog?"

"No. Why?"

"He chewed through that wire fence and escaped. We can't find him anyplace. If Josh is right about him having rabies..."

Tanner didn't finish, but he didn't need to do that. Josh felt a shiver of fear race up and down his arms. *A possibly rabid dog loose in this place!*

Chapter Seven

A DANGEROUS PLAN

Back in camp Tanner pointed out where Maka had escaped. Several strands of the cage's stout wire gate had been gnawed through and pushed out at the lower left side. Hairs showed where the dog had squeezed through.

Tank's voice held disbelief. "It doesn't seem possible that any animal could have chewed through such heavy fencing. It must have hurt him a lot, judging from the blood on the ends of those wires."

"Well, that's what Maka did," Keoni said. He looked around. "I wonder where he is."

The sergeant shifted his rifle and glanced around. "We've looked everywhere without any luck. So don't go anyplace alone, especially after dark."

Josh frowned. *How can we check out the boat tonight with a possibly rabid dog on the loose?* Aloud, he warned, "Don't touch anything around Maka's cage. If he does have rabies, we can't take any chances on getting infected." He paused, thinking fast. "Come to think of it, I'm pretty sure

65

that anyone who's handled a rabid animal is supposed to get shots just to be safe. But I'd have to check the encyclopedia to be sure."

"We've all touched Maka!" Keoni exclaimed.

"All except Josh and Tank," his sister added.

Tanner nodded. "I've already read the encyclopedia, Josh, and you're right. But the lieutenant says he doesn't believe the dog is infected."

"But we can't take that chance!" Josh cried. "I'll go talk to him."

"No, Josh!" Pua exclaimed. "I'd better do that."

"Okay, but I'll go with you," Josh replied.

Pua hesitated, then nodded. "Let me do the talking. Keoni, you stay close to Sergeant Tanner."

"Don't upset your father!" Tanner warned. "He's already a little huhu with me because of what I've said."

Tank decided, "I'll check on my dad."

Outside the flap of the lieutenant's tent, Pua called softly, "Daddy, may I come in?"

"Who's there?" the voice was harsh.

"Oh, no!" Pua breathed, her brown eyes widening with concern as she looked at Josh. "I think he's having another of his spells."

The tent flap was moved back with the point of a cutlass. Josh instinctively stepped back as the gleaming blade held the canvas aside. Pua's father was dressed exactly like the one-legged pirate Josh had first seen on the black-sand beach.

"Who dares disturb Captain Kidd by coming to his quarters without being summoned?" he roared, taking an awkward step on the wooden leg.

"Daddy, it's me!" Pua's voice showed alarm.

Josh's instincts warned him to back up or run, but he couldn't leave Pua in danger. He started to speak, but she suddenly gripped his hand and squeezed it in a warning to let her handle the matter.

"Well, now," the man said, his voice softening a little. "The master of a stout vessel never allows a maid on his ship. It's bad luck. But ye seem to be a comely lass. What are ye called?"

"Oh, Daddy, don't you know me? I'm Pua."

The man frowned and stared down at the girl for a long moment. "Tell Mr. Hook he has the watch," he finally said. "I'll be in me quarters." He took a clumsy step backward into the tent and lowered the cutlass. The tent flap fell into place.

Josh gulped and took a long, slow breath of air, then blew it out noisily.

Pua looked at him, her eyes glistening with sudden tears. "We've got to do something—fast!" she said hoarsely. She turned away from the tent and started walking rapidly across the open area. "Josh, please have everyone meet me at the table right away."

Josh hurried to Tanner and Keoni and delivered the girl's message. As they moved toward the table, Josh ran to Sam Catlett's tent. He had moved his cot back inside.

"How do you feel, Mr. Catlett?" Josh asked.

"My head still hurts, and my leg is getting mighty sore. But I'll be all right."

Tank explained in a low voice. "His fever's starting up. He thinks it's from his leg getting infected by the coral cut. But when he asked for a thermometer, he was told that there isn't one around."

Josh began to feel overwhelmed at the troubles piling up around him. He instantly resisted, reminding himself to trust in God. Josh quickly explained what had just happened at the lieutenant's tent, and Pua's request.

Mr. Catlett mused, "So now Beacher thinks he's Captain Kidd again? Awhile ago we were exchanging war stories, and he was as rational as we are. However, he did get a little emotional when he found out I flew helicopters in 'Nam. He told me that he owed his life to one of us."

"Oh? What happened?" Josh asked.

"It seems he was badly wounded in the jungles, and the chopper pilot hovered over a little clearing to lift him out. At the time, the helicopter was taking small-arms fire. Because I was assigned to the area where he was picked up, he wondered if I was the pilot who'd rescued him. We were just starting to discuss that possibility when Tanner ran in, saying the dog had disappeared."

"I'd like to hear more, Mr. Catlett," Josh said, "but we have to go. We'll be back as soon as we can."

As the boys left the tent, Tank moaned. "I'm afraid he'll

die if we don't find some way to get help for him!" Tank shot
a hard look toward the lieutenant's tent. "I'm starting to hate
that man! He has to see that Dad needs outside medical help!"

"Mr. Beacher can't really help himself, Tank. One minute
he thinks he's a pirate, and the next he's an army lieutenant.
Maybe now Pua will decide to help us. If not, we'll find a
way to check out the boat tonight."

"Oh, sure!" Tank said with mock sarcasm. "We just walk
through the jungle with no flashlight and a rabid dog running
loose!" Tank shook his head vigorously. "We'll have to look
for the boat in daylight and pray we don't run into the dog or
the sergeant."

Josh reluctantly agreed as he and Tank approached the
table where Tanner, Pua, and her brother were seated. Their
voices were raised in argument.

"I can't do it, Pua!" the sergeant exclaimed.

"Not even if it means risking all our lives, including your
own?" she snapped.

"He's the best superior officer I ever knew!" the sergeant
said with feeling. "When your father comes out of this thing,
I'll talk to him again. Whatever decision he makes then, and
whatever orders he gives, I'll obey."

Keoni exclaimed, "You're not in the army anymore!"

Tanner didn't answer, but strode away with the rifle.

Josh said, "Keoni, maybe in his mind, Sergeant Tanner
really is still in the army."

Keoni agreed. "Maybe so." He looked pale, and his eyes

were wide with concern.

Josh and Tank sat down at the table across from Pua and Keoni.

Pua explained, "I wanted the sergeant to take the boat and run down the coast to Hilo and get help," she explained to Josh and Tank. "He's so loyal to Daddy that sometimes I wonder which of them has the most trouble with their thinking."

"What are we going to do now?" Keoni asked sadly. "Maka's out there somewhere in the jungle, maybe biting all kinds of animals and spreading rabies like crazy. He could bite us too!"

Tank said quietly, "My dad's getting worse. He has to have a doctor."

"I know," Josh answered. He turned to Keoni. "Why don't you go stick close to the sergeant while Tank and I talk with your sister alone."

"I want to stay and talk too," he protested.

Pua gave his fingers a squeeze. "You'd better do as Josh said. And don't worry."

After her brother left, the girl looked at Josh and Tank. "I told him, 'Don't worry!' but I'm a fine one to talk. I'm worried out of my mind."

"Look, Pua," Josh began. "We need to have outside medical help here, and fast. Now, if you'll help us find some way to signal for help…"

"The sergeant won't let you near the beach," she

interrupted with a shake of her head.

Tank grabbed Josh's arm and looked earnestly into his eyes. "Let's tell her."

"Tell me what?" she asked.

Josh explained, "We know where the boat is. We could take that..."

Pua interrupted. "That won't work, because Daddy has the key. He keeps it with him."

Tank sagged forward onto the table with a low groan.

Josh felt like doing the same, but he fought back his sense of disappointment. He looked straight at Pua. "If you want to save everybody's lives, then help us think of another way to get help in a hurry!"

Pua studied him thoughtfully for a long moment, then commented, "Daddy walked into this place."

"I know," Josh replied. "But he said there's no way somebody could do that now because of the booby traps."

Pua chewed her lips, her eyes never leaving Josh's. "There is a way," she said in a very low voice. "It's dangerous, but not from booby traps. They're hidden because Daddy's afraid someone else might walk in here, just as he did."

Josh frowned. "I don't understand."

"This is a small valley, so getting out of it is the easy part. That is, *if* you know where to walk. The real danger comes after. You see, the trail leads through some old lava flows. Naturally, nobody lives there. And, since the volcano started erupting a few days ago, one of the rifts could suddenly open right under a person's feet."

Josh had to force himself to answer calmly. "If that's the only way," he said, "I'll go."

Tank said thoughtfully, "I want to go with you, but I'd better stay to take care of my dad."

Pua stood up, then leaned forward to put her palms flat on the table. She looked down at Tank sitting across the table from her. "I'll take care of your father. You'd better go with Josh so if you run into trouble, you can help each other."

"But Dad's my responsibility!" Tank protested.

Pua said firmly, "I can do as much or more than you, so you go with Josh." She paused and sat back down. "I mean, if you're willing to do that."

"Of course I'm willing," Tank assured her.

Josh said, "I think Tank should stay with his dad."

"Believe me," Pua said emphatically, "we'll all have a better chance if you go together."

Tank pursed his lips thoughtfully. "I'll talk it over with my dad." He stood up.

Josh got to his feet. "I'll go with you, Tank."

The boys explained the proposal to Mr. Catlett. He listened in silence until they'd finished. "That trip could be very dangerous for you boys," he said thoughtfully. "But for all of us to stay here under the circumstances is no good either. Come closer and let's pray about it."

When Mr. Catlett had finished, Josh said firmly, "I want to go, so I'll go alone."

"I can't let you do that," Tank protested. "You heard what Pua said. It's too dangerous for one person."

"Her father did it," Josh reminded him.

Mr. Catlett said, "But he's a grown man, and a veteran of the Vietnam jungles, trained in survival. I hate the idea of either of you boys risking your lives on a walk out of here."

"But, Dad," Tank protested, "I'm more scared of what might happen if you don't get to a doctor soon. Maybe I'd better go with Josh."

When the boys rejoined Pua and announced their decision, she looked around to be sure nobody else was near. "I thought you'd do that," she said. "I've drawn a map. Later, I'll leave a couple canteens of water, some food, and a couple of ponchos* inside your tent. Sit down and we'll go over this map together."

As the boys took bench seats on both sides of the girl, Tank asked, "Why the ponchos?"

Pua unfolded the map and pointed at what she'd drawn. "You're starting from the shore here, and there's no road or much of anything until you reach Highway 11. That's quite a ways inland. When you get out of this valley, you'll be climbing partway up Mauna Loa,* which is more than 13,000 feet high. When you start climbing, you'll have cold and rainy weather, even though you're on an active volcano."

Josh explained, "We were flying over Kilauea Iki* on the side of that mountain when our engine quit. That's the Hawaii Volcanoes National Park, with all kinds of old lava flows and vents that were spouting lava high into the air."

Pua assured him, "You shouldn't have to go very far before you see somebody or find a phone."

Josh studied the map. "We're a long way from Hilo or any town I recognize."

"That's why you'll have to figure on finding Highway 11. That goes from Kailua-Kona* over here on the left, around the south end of the island to Naalahu.* It's only about 65 miles from there to Hilo, so you should see cars on that highway when you find it."

"My father drove us that way one time," Tank commented. "It's slow going."

"Yes," Pua agreed. "but you might run across somebody before you reach the highway. If not, you'll see cars on it. Just don't get lost, and watch out for rift vents. They sometimes open up unexpectedly far from the actual crater and throw lava into the air."

"We'll watch out, and we'll travel light," Josh said. "So we won't need the water. There'll be fresh streams along the way."

"Maybe," Pua admitted, smoothing out the small sheet of lined notebook paper. "But if wild hogs have wallowed in it, you could pick up some germs and become sick. Better drink only our water. We get it from the waterfall, which comes from the rain over the mountains."

When the boys nodded, Pua continued. "I'll wrap up a little rice to eat. But you'd better save it until you get to the lava flows. In the valley there's plenty of wild bananas, guavas,* lilikoi*—you haoles* call it passion fruit—and other wild fruit to eat. Now, let me explain this map."

When she had finished, Pua looked quickly toward her father's tent, and then to where her brother and the sergeant were cautiously searching for signs of the dog at the end of the camp.

"It's too late to start now," Pua declared, "and you'd never make it in the dark without a light. So you'd better plan on leaving first thing in the morning."

Josh asked, "What about the sergeant and your father?"

"I'll find an excuse to get their attention somewhere else. Then you two take off and follow the trail I've marked. Don't stray off of it, because you could run into a booby trap."

As the boys nodded, Pua continued, "You won't have any weapons, so watch out for Maka. He could be anywhere. And finally, you'll be chased, so go fast."

"Chased?" Josh and Tank repeated together.

Pua nodded. "Daddy will almost surely send the sergeant after you. The sergeant would love that. Sometimes he pretends he's back in the Vietnam jungles hunting down the enemy. Believe me, you don't want him to catch you!"

Chapter Eight

JUNGLE JEOPARDY

Tank protested, "Sergeant Tanner knows us, and he's been pretty nice. You don't think he'd ...?"

"I don't know," Pua interrupted. "But remember, you're not dealing with someone who thinks like most people. He could do something terrible to you. But even if he brought you back here, it might be too late for Tank's father, and maybe for the rest of us too."

"You're scaring me!" Tank said.

Pua replied crisply, "If you don't want to go..."

Josh quickly interrupted, "We're going! We just wish there was an easier way."

"Me too," Pua agreed. "But there isn't. Now, if you can keep the sergeant from catching you, your biggest dangers will be from nature. I mean, slippery footing on volcanic rocks, wild hogs, and anything from the volcano. Even the gasses can be poisonous, so try to stay upwind of any venting, eruption, or anything like that. Don't forget that you're racing the clock too."

Josh swallowed hard, fighting the demons of doubt that attacked his mind like a school of piranhas.* He stood up. "We'll be careful, and we'll go fast," he promised. "You keep an eye open for Maka. Don't let him bite anybody."

"Thanks for taking care of my dad," Tank added.

Josh folded the map, put it in his pants pocket, and said a silent prayer.

Dawn was barely breaking the next morning when Josh and Tank slipped barefooted out of their tent. Tank tiptoed to his father's tent to check on him. Then, without even a whispered word to each other, the boys carried their heavy walking boots along with the canteens of water, the packages, and the stout sticks that Pua had left for them.

Barely breathing in their efforts to be quiet, the boys skirted the cages so the birds and animals wouldn't set up an alarm that might awaken the other people. Once out of camp, the boys headed toward the mountain range at the far end of the pocket valley.

As they entered the rain forest a quarter mile from the camp, Tank whispered, "I hope these sticks are strong enough to defend us from Maka if we run across him."

Josh nodded, shivering at what it would mean if the dog was rabid and attacked him and Tank. "I'll watch for him while you put your boots on," Josh said. "Then you do the same for me."

Every nerve in Josh's body remained alert while Tank pulled on his hiking boots. Then Josh did the same, but his eyes apprehensively swept every bush and shadow.

After slipping out of camp, they made good time, passing through the rain forest without seeing anything more exciting than some rats and several giant, six-inch-long African snails. Both boys were relieved when they reached an open area with scattered wild guava, papaya,* mango,* and banana trees.

Josh glanced back as the shadows retreated from the light of day. There was no sign of Tanner following and no indication that Maka was anywhere around.

"Hungry?" Josh asked in a low voice. "There're some lilikoi vines with ripe fruit just ahead."

"I'm too revved up to eat." Tank squinted at a guava tree with its rounded, yellowish fruit within easy reach. Some had already fallen to the ground. "But maybe I'll take some of those along to eat later."

"Something's been eating those on the ground. See?"

"Wild pigs, maybe," Tank guessed, examining the half-eaten fruit. "Those pigs love guavas."

Josh looked around with some concern. "My dad says wild pigs weight up to 300 or 400 pounds, but they're not usually aggressive."

"Even so, I don't want to run into them." Tank straightened up from examining the guavas on the ground. "Let's get out of here."

As the boys hurried on, Josh explained, "Dad said these feral* pigs—that's what he calls them—are descendants of domestic animals that had been turned loose or escaped many years ago. I know some kids at our apartments who've seen wild pigs that live in the Koolau Range behind Honolulu."

Josh concluded, "The male hogs have tusks that curve up, so they can slash a person's legs to ribbons."

"I sure hope we don't run into one of them," Tank said fervently.

Hurrying on, occasionally checking their back trail for signs of the sergeant and keeping a wary eye out for the dog, the boys approached a tiny stream that emerged from porous basaltic* rock. Josh produced the map Pua had drawn for them.

"So far, so good," Josh commented, replacing the map. "The water looks good. Want a drink?"

"Not yet."

The boys started to pass the stream. Suddenly Josh stopped and pointed. "It's muddy. Probably means that pigs were wading in it minutes ago, because it's not cleared yet."

"I see tracks over there." Tank took a couple of quick steps and bent to look closer. "They're the tracks, all right—a big one and some little ones. Hey!" His voice shot up in alarm. "Dog tracks too!"

Josh felt his heart speed up as he quickly examined the ground. "Sure is! They have to be Maka's. And those different-size pig tracks has to mean a mother hog with her little ones." Josh gripped his stick tighter and looked fearfully around. There was no sign of either dog or pigs. He dropped his voice. "Don't talk any more! Let's run as quietly as we can and keep our eyes open!"

The boys broke into a trot, their eyes flickering about in search of the dog or pigs.

As the boys were passing a dense growth of lilikoi vines, their base seemed to explode. A mottled white sow squealed with fury and charged both boys.

Josh yelled in terror, "Look out!" He dropped Pua's package and the heavy stick while desperately looking around for some form of safety. He grabbed the lilikoi vines over his head.

Tank also dropped his stick and package to seize another vine. He jerked his feet up out of harm's way. The sow's momentum carried her past him, but she stopped abruptly and swung around with horrible clicking teeth.

"Get your feet onto the vines!" Josh yelled, not thinking that the sergeant might be following and would hear him.

"I'm... trying!" Tank bent at the waist and swung his legs upward.

The sow, still squealing furiously, slashed at the base of the vines where Tank clung. Suddenly, the one that Tank clung to broke with a terrifying snap.

"Ohhhhh!" Tank shrieked, frantically letting go of the broken vine and grabbing for another.

As Josh watched in helpless fear, Tank's fingers closed about a second vine. His fall was broken, but his feet swung inches above the ground.

The sow, weighing at least 200 pounds, was surprisingly

fast. Her little eyes glittered as she again charged toward Tank's dangling legs.

"Help me!" Tank screamed, desperately trying to get his legs up out of the way.

Josh didn't think; he just acted. He let go of the vines and dropped, landing on his knees in the trail. He snatched up the stick he'd dropped, knowing it was of little use against the big animal.

"Hey!" Josh yelled as loud as he could. He swung the stick and advanced toward the sow. She stopped slashing at Tank's feet just as he pulled them safely out of reach in the vines. The sow grunted and faced Josh.

"You crazy?" Tank called from his perch in the vines. "Get away from her!" Josh started to back up toward his vine, still yelling and striking toward the sow with the stick. Josh thought for one hopeful moment that the hog would turn and vanish into the undergrowth.

Then, from behind him, Josh heard the squeal of a little pig. Too late, Josh realized he was between the angry mother and the brood she was protecting.

With a vicious grunt, the sow again charged Josh.

He had never realized how fast a hog could move. The sow's angry squeals and clicking teeth warned him that he couldn't just stand there, yet the sight of the furious charge seemed to root Josh to the trail.

Tank's frantic voice from the lilikoi vines roused Josh. "Climb! Climb!"

Josh turned and leaped upward, reaching as high as he could into the vines. He heard the sow grunt just below and glanced down in time to see her make a lunge for his legs. Josh frantically jerked them out of the way, but not before the hog's teeth slashed at him.

She got me! Josh's mind screamed as his right leg snapped violently away with a sound of jeans tearing. Josh bent his knees so that both feet were raised out of the animal's reach. As the sow struck repeatedly at the vines with her snout, Josh glanced fearfully at his leg.

The pants leg had been ripped open. There was no sign of blood, although he could feel where the teeth had found his calf just above his boot top. He felt no pain, but Josh knew that shock sometimes momentarily masked the agony of a fresh wound.

Fearfully, Josh released his hold on the vines with one hand and used the other to pull up the tattered remnant of jeans. Josh stared at his bare flesh.

From his nearby vine, Tank asked, "How bad is it?"

"I've got long red streaks, but she didn't break the skin! Another fraction of an inch deeper and..." he stopped with a shudder.

"Now what do we do?" Tank asked.

"We wait. If she thinks her litter's safe, she'll soon go off—I hope."

The sow made a halfhearted charge toward the boys. Then, apparently satisfied that she had won the encounter, she trotted off. She was followed by a litter of pigs ranging in color from very black to spotted to a dirty white. They vanished into the underbrush.

After awhile, the boys retrieved their sticks and Pua's packages, then resumed their trek at a fast walk.

Tank said softly, "You did a dumb thing in trying to help me back there, but—thanks."

Josh playfully punched his friend in the shoulder. "You've saved me more than once. Only do me a favor: don't get into that kind of a mess again."

"I won't! You can count on that."

"We've still got to be careful," Josh cautioned as the sun rose over the mountain ridge to the right. "Maka may still be somewhere close by, and if the sergeant is following us, then he must have heard all the shouting and commotion."

"Let's make tracks," Tank urged.

The boys hurried on, eventually reaching a beautiful verdant area filled mostly with ti plants ranging up to ten feet tall.

Josh admired the versatile plants that Hawaiians used for many purposes. That included so-called "grass skirts," thatched houses, and as drinking cups or plates from which to eat.

Where's Maka? Josh wondered, as fast-moving clouds overhead hinted at the possibility of one of Hawaii's sudden, light showers. Beneath the clouds, a line of kukui trees with pale green leaves grew in a gulch. A moment later, a rainbow formed low over the trees.

It was so beautiful that Josh momentarily forgot the urgency of his mission. He was brought back to that problem by his friend's sad voice.

"You think my dad's going to be okay?"

"Sure," Josh said with a cheerfulness he didn't feel. "And Pua's father will get the help he needs when we get out of here and find a phone or somebody." He glanced around, then pulled out the map again.

"Pua shows a little waterfall where we're to turn left. But here we have two waterfalls. Maybe she forgot to draw the other."

"Yeah, or maybe we're lost."

"I hope not." Josh looked around thoughtfully. "Well, we can't stand here thinking about it. We're probably far enough that the dog's still not a threat to us, but the sergeant sure is. So which way do we go?"

"Let's see that map again."

After studying it carefully, Josh debated with himself. "Left, I think," he decided.

Tank, always willing to follow, nodded.

Josh had a vaguely uneasy feeling that they had somehow made a wrong turn. He silently fretted about blundering into a booby trap.

The boys were nearing the end of the pocket valley when far behind they heard several shots. They stopped and looked back the way they'd come.

"What do you think?" Tank asked in a low voice. "Was

that the sergeant shooting?"

"Has to be, because we're pretty far from camp. But what was he shooting at? The sow? The dog? Or what?"

Tank shrugged. "Well, we know for sure that he's on our trail, so it doesn't matter what he was firing at, does it?"

Josh shook his head. "No, because the next time, it could be us, unless we can lose him." Josh hurriedly pulled out the map. "If we're still heading the right way, when we cross this little mountain range, we'll come to some old lava flows. They'll be very hard going."

"You're telling me! Remember the time we walked out to that fire pit? That old lava is so sharp it cut our tennis shoes to pieces."

Josh remembered that the walk had been worth it, for they'd stood at the edge of an open pit filled with reddish molten lava. It sloshed about, making a moaning sound like a giant animal in pain.

Josh refolded the map and replaced it in his pants pocket. "Walking over old lava flows is a lot better than having the sergeant catch us."

The boys walked on to dry country where thorny kiawe* grew on the side of the low mountain. They carefully picked their way around the tangled barrier, emerging with only minor scratches on their arms.

They again checked their trail, but didn't see or hear any sign of pursuit. *But,* Josh admitted to himself with some concern, *I'm sure the sergeant's following us.*

The terrain had totally changed. In the distance, the unmistakable mass of Mauna Loa rose majestically toward the sky. On its lower right-hand slope lay the Hawaii Volcanoes National Park with Kilauea Iki's active volcano. Somewhere out there, unseen from the boys' position, Highway 11 ran inland from the sea to pass to the top of Kilauea Iki. The City of Hilo was many miles to the right. But from where the boys stood, they could see only the bulk of the great volcanic mountain and the desolation that lay between.

Old, very rough black lava spread ahead and on both sides. The only signs of life were a few small, green plants that had somehow managed to find enough soil in cracks to grow upward a few inches. A few dead, twisted skeletons of burned trees remained standing in the endless volcanic blackness.

Tank sniffed noisily. "Smell that?"

Josh became aware of the faint odor on the wind. "That's sulphur from the volcano." He shaded his eyes from the morning sun and studied the horizon. "Can't see anything, but it's definitely still erupting."

"We'd better stay away from it." Tank turned to the right, then the left. "Hey! We're still close to the shoreline. Look over there."

Josh followed his friend's pointing hand to the left. "I hate to admit it," he said with concern. "I think we should be much farther inland—at least, that's the way I read Pua's map."

"How could we be lost if we've found this little mountain

with all the kiawe? It's on her map."

"I don't know." Josh studied the volcanic cliffs where an ancient lava flow had spilled into the ocean. "But I'm sure we shouldn't have come out this close to the ocean. We should be much further inland."

"You mean, we really are lost?"

Josh thoughtfully examined the map before answering. "I'm not sure. Pua's directions got us safely out of the valley." Josh stuck the map back in his pocket. "Wherever we are, it's right in the middle of nowhere."

Suddenly, Tank suddenly grabbed his arm. "Look!"

Josh spun around in alarm.

Sergeant Tanner, carrying his rifle, was just emerging from the tangle of kiawe trees!

Chapter Nine

A DESPERATE CHASE

Josh sucked in his breath at sight of the sergeant and his rifle. The barrel had caught in some thorny kiawe. Then, Josh reacted. "Get down!" he hissed, pushing Tank's shoulder hard. "Maybe he hasn't seen us!"

The boys dropped their packages and sticks into a small depression about two feet deep made by the hard, rough lava. Then they followed, throwing themselves down and skinning their hands and knees on the basalt rock.*

Josh, holding his breath, listened hard for sounds of their pursuer's footsteps. Instead, Josh heard only the distant noise of the ocean. It kept up a constant roar, sounding like a freight train that never passed. The trade winds ruffled Josh's brown hair, making him try to get even lower in the depression.

After what seemed like forever, Josh raised his head just enough to look into Tank's face. It was pale under his light blond hair. His eyes were wide with fright.

"If he catches us," Tank whispered so softly that Josh could barely hear, "my father could die!"

Josh nodded, thinking, *And so could Pua and Keoni if Maka really does have rabies!* "We have to get away," Josh whispered back. "We've just got to!"

"Yes, but how? If we run across that open lava, the sergeant could shoot us!"

"I'm sure he won't do that. He and Lieutenant Beacher just want to keep us from letting anyone know about their secrets at Pirate's Point. So the sergeant will try to catch us and take us back to camp."

"If that happens, I'm afraid my dad will die!"

Josh didn't answer, but suspected that Tank was probably right. Josh again strained to hear if the sergeant's footsteps were coming this way. As before, Josh heard only the steady roar of the ocean.

He leaned closer to whisper in Tank's ear. "I'm going to take another peek. You stay down, okay?"

As Tank nodded, Josh carefully raised his head. He stopped when his eyes came even with the top of the depression. Tanner had a pack on his back and carried the rifle. He crouched low, moving to the left, parallel to the kiawe growing on the side of the mountain.

"He's going the other way," Josh reported, dropping back down beside his friend. "Maybe we can slip out of here and head the other direction."

"But that'll take us along the cliffs above the ocean! We've got to cross the lava flows to the highway."

"Right now, we've got to keep out of Sergeant Tanner's

way," Josh replied grimly. "We'll circle back to the highway after we lose him." The boy again cautiously raised his head enough to see that the sergeant was still moving away.

Josh turned back to Tank to report, "He's maybe a quarter mile away. Let's go."

"Maybe we should just stay still until he's a lot farther away."

"What if he turns and comes back?" Josh peeped over the top of his shelter again, then slowly turned and looked all around. "He's still heading away." Josh gathered up his package and gripped his stick.

"Our best bet is to stay low and try to get back by the kiawe trees. They're not much protection, but they're better than nothing. Follow the trees to where the mountain ends and the lava cliffs begin. They're full of ledges and maybe some lava tubes. If we can find one of those, we can just hide in there until it's safe. Come on."

Josh's lips moved in earnest silent prayer as he bent low and led the way back across the few feet of tumbled black basalt toward the line of kiawe. The ancient lava flow, when it was red-black and moved like melting blobs of ugly butter, had divided at the small mountainous ridge. The magma had poured around both ends into the sea, leaving soil where some kiawe trees now stood more than 30 feet tall.

Josh was grateful when he and Tank reached the sparse shelter of the nearest trees and crouched low. They caught their breaths, which were irregular more from fear than exertion. They spotted the sergeant in the distance, still moving away.

Josh said with satisfaction, "So far, so good. Now if we can just get down those little cliffs where he can't see us, we can stand up and make better time."

"We've got to make it!" Tank answered. "Everything depends on it!"

Josh led the way to the end of the little mountain and the beginning of the lava flow that had spilled into the sea in times past. Breathing hard, Josh turned and looked back. "The sergeant's gone!"

"Yeah! But where did he go? Down the cliffs? Or did he see us and turn back to follow us? It's possible that he's hiding in some little place as we were, watching for us to show ourselves."

"Don't say that!"

"Either way, we have to keep moving." Josh stood at the top of the cliff and looked down. There was no beach, just tumbled black masses of basalt that glistened silvery in the sun. *There's no way we can walk down there,* he told himself with keen disappointment. *And we can't stay up here where the sergeant can see us.*

"Over there!" Tank exclaimed, gripping Josh's arm. "See that little ledge leading to what looks like the opening of an old lava tube? Maybe we could hide there."

"Let's try it." Josh started down, followed by Tank. Josh needed both hands to keep from falling into the surging waves below. He dropped his stick, stuffed Pua's package inside his shirt, and eased down the cliff.

The rough basaltic rocks had made Josh's fingers bleed by the time he had lowered himself 10 or 12 feet. When his feet touched the small ledge, he let out a relieved sigh.

Followed by Tank, Josh walked carefully along the rough trail to where a three-foot-wide opening revealed a lava tube. Long ago, molten red-hot rock had shot out from the tube like water from a giant garden hose to sizzle and solidify under the surf.

"Looks okay," Josh announced, peering into the tube. "It's about 30 feet long, but I can't see out the back. We can stay here until it's safe."

Tank squeezed in beside Josh, saying, "The sergeant will never find us here. We didn't leave any tracks on that lava, so he can't follow us now."

Josh scowled, suddenly remembering something. "Our sticks! What'd you do with yours?"

"Dropped it beside yours. Why?"

"That kind of stick isn't found along here. If Tanner finds them, he might even recognize they're from camp. Then he'd guess we went this way. We saw this opening, so he can too."

"We'd better get out of here!"

"I don't know which is more risky," Josh said thoughtfully, "trying to go on along those cliffs where we could fall in the surf and get pounded to death, or staying here hoping Tanner doesn't find us. I'm going to crawl back to the end of this tube and see if we can get out that way."

A dusty smell filled Josh's nostrils as he crawled away from the tube's entrance where moisture from the ocean drifted in. Instead of the tube getting darker as he eased deeper into it, he glimpsed faint light ahead.

A moment later he stopped in surprise. "Hey!" he called softly, his voice echoing. "It's open at the back!"

The exit was much smaller, but Josh figured he and Tank could squeeze through. Still, before committing himself fully, Josh inched forward until he could see that the exit faced another solid basalt cliff. In between, there was an open area like a small ravine.

Sticking his head out for a better look, Josh saw that there was a narrow valley about ten feet wide between two black cliffs at least 30 feet high.

He drew in his head and explained, "There's a little dry gully going off to the right. I can't see the end, but we'd better find out where it goes."

"Anything's better than sitting here like rats in a cage, waiting for the sergeant to come get us."

The sun was now high overhead, shining directly down into the canyon-like area. "Lava sure does strange things," Josh commented, moving along the trail. "Looks like rain water has smoothed this out from running down to the sea for so many years."

"Don't talk!" Tank whispered from two steps behind. "These walls may magnify our voices so the sergeant can hear us."

The boys moved as silently as possible, their heavy walking boots making the only sound as they followed the strange formation. Josh glanced up and realized the sun had seemed to shift position slightly. Because very little time had passed, he knew they were changing direction. He tried to listen for the surf, but no sound reached the bottom of the narrow canyon.

Josh led the way around a corner, then stopped abruptly. "Wow!" he breathed. "Look at that!"

The cliffs on both sides started to converge less than 200 yards away to form a box canyon. At the far end, a large bowl-shaped impression showed that water had once been impounded there. Josh lifted his eyes and saw where a waterfall about 200 feet above had dried up. Everything was very dry, rough, and broken.

Tank said softly but with feeling, "I'm not going in there. I'm already beginning to feel like these cliffs are closing in on me."

Josh sensed some claustrophobia himself, but he didn't want to say that. *We're trapped*, he thought. *We can't go past that dead end, but we heard the sergeant behind us. If we turn back, we'll probably run into him. Yet we're losing too much time sitting here.*

"Let's go forward," he suggested to Tank. "Let's see if there's some way we can climb out."

"Climb out to what? Have the sergeant catch us?"

Josh didn't answer, guessing that Tank was frustrated

with the knowledge that his father's condition probably was getting worse while precious time slid silently by.

At the end, Josh had to fight his feeling of claustrophobia, for the three sides closed in until they met in a narrow point not more than a foot wide.

He looked up, judging whether it would be possible to climb out 200 or 300 feet to the top of the box canyon.

What's up there? Maybe we'll step right out in front of the sergeant. But if we stay down here, we're never going to find somebody to help us.

As Josh silently debated with himself, he heard a single shot fired behind him. He glanced back the way they'd come as the sound of the rifle echoed off the basalt walls and faded into the distance.

Josh and Tank looked at each other.

"How close do you think that was?" Tank asked in a weak, croaking voice. "And what'd he shoot at?"

"I don't have any idea," Josh answered both questions at once. "But it was near enough to know he's closing in on us."

Josh again looked straight up. "The only way out of here is to climb this cliff," he said grimly. "But it's maybe a couple of hundred feet. If we fall..." he left the terrible thought unfinished.

"The sergeant could easily see us on that wall!"

"But we don't have any choice except to keep climbing, do we?" Josh reached up and gripped the rough black lava.

Tank muttered under his breath, "Sometimes I wish I had

a best friend who didn't always get into trouble."

Josh felt a weak smile tugging at his lips in spite of their situation. "You going to talk or climb?" he asked good-naturedly.

"If we fall, nobody'll ever find us," Tank commented, reaching up to follow Josh.

They moved in silence, hand over hand, until Josh judged they'd reached 50 feet or so above the narrow rocky trail. *I wish we'd thought to bring a rope.*

Such a spooky feeling began to seep over Josh that he glanced around nervously. *What's the matter with you?* he scolded himself. *There's nothing to be afraid of here, except falling, or the sergeant. At least Maka can't bother us on this cliff.*

The spooky feeling became stronger. Josh tried to shake it off, but it wouldn't leave. He saw a ledge sticking out about a foot from the cliff barely three feet ahead.

"I've got to rest and catch my breath," he told Tank. Josh followed his words by glancing down, and nearly loosened his hold on the rough lava. "Don't look down!" Josh warned, gulping at how far they'd climbed.

"I don't like heights," Tank puffed, still climbing. "Especially this high. If my dad wasn't so bad off, I'd never do this."

"Me neither," Josh agreed. He rested until Tank was only about a yard below, then Josh took a deep breath, fought down his anxiety, and started climbing again.

He reached the basalt ledge that stuck out a foot or so from the cliff's face. Josh carefully felt with his fingers until he had a secure grip. *It's going to be harder climbing past that ledge,* he warned himself. *Mustn't slip.*

Cautiously, Josh tested his hold, then pushed with his booted feet against the cliff below and pulled hard with his hands on the protruding shelf.

Puffing hard, he pulled himself up until his eyes were even with the top of the ledge.

"Oh!" he cried in terror, nearly losing his grip.

He stared into the empty eye sockets of a human skull just inches away.

Chapter Ten

STRANGE HIDING PLACES

With a shudder Josh turned his face away from the scary object on the ledge.

Below him, Tank asked urgently, "What's the matter?"

"There's a human skull up here! It looks as if it's grinning at me."

"A skull? It can't hurt you!" Tank scoffed.

"My head knows that, but my heart doesn't. It's racing like mad!"

"You'd better be more scared of the sergeant," Tank warned, starting to climb again. "Let me look up there."

Josh started to feel a little foolish at his fear. He forced himself to turn and face the skull. This time, it didn't look so terrifying. Josh's gaze swept past it.

"Hey, there's another one! Two, three—a whole bunch of them! And skeletons. There's a shallow depression, like a cave, filled with them."

Tank's head appeared above the ridge, level with Josh's. Tank asked in awe, "You know what this must be?"

Josh nodded. "My father told me that the ancient

Hawaiians used to bury their dead in caves and places like this, especially their royalty, the alii."*

Tank counted softly, "Seven of them. They must have been here for centuries."

Josh's speeding heart slowed to normal. "I never expected to come face to face with anything like this. But it's better than meeting the sergeant."

Josh looked down the way they'd come. "From the sound of that last shot, we know he's closing in on us. But he can't find us if we hide up here on this ledge."

"Hide here with these? No way!"

"Now who's afraid?" Josh chided. "But we can either do that, or hang onto this cliff until the sergeant sees us."

Tank's familiar groan echoed off the shallow burial chamber. "If it weren't for my father..."

"I know," Josh replied, carefully hoisting himself onto the ledge between the two nearest skulls. "We'll let the sergeant pass, then we'll climb down and go back the way we came. After that, we'll cut straight across the lava flows toward the highway and find some help."

In respect and awe, the boys cautiously eased past the human remains. Stealing uneasy glances at the skeletons, Josh and Tank gently placed their backs against the wall of the shallow depression. That gave them a view of the way they'd come, so they could see the sergeant if he passed below.

The minutes dragged on with no sign of pursuit while the friends silently fretted about losing valuable time.

Josh's stomach growled in the eerie silence, so he

remembered the packages Pua had given them. But he didn't have any appetite, not with seven skeletons around him.

"How do you suppose these got down here?" Josh mused. "Nobody could have carried them."

When Tank didn't reply, Josh suggested, "They must have lowered them from the top of this cliff. But I don't think the ancient Hawaiians had ropes. So could they have found or made vines long enough for that?"

"There he comes!" Tank exclaimed, grabbing Josh's arm. "See? I didn't think he could follow us through that lava tube, but he's coming the exact way we did!"

"Shh!" Josh cautioned, bending forward so there was no chance of being seen if the sergeant happened to look up to the burial ledge. *He's a mighty good tracker,* Josh grudgingly admitted. *But he can't be good enough to see where we started climbing.*

The pursuer disappeared under the burial ledge so the boys couldn't see him directly below. Josh held his breath and strained to hear. *Is he climbing after us? I can't hear him, but maybe I won't. Maybe the first time we'll know is when his face appears....*

Josh's thoughts were interrupted by Tank's sudden grip on his arm. "There," Tank whispered, pointing to the left and down. "He's passed us."

"Thank God!" Josh exclaimed softly, aware that he had been tense for so long that his body ached.

The boys waited for several minutes after Tanner had disappeared. Then they gladly left the burial ledge and quickly climbed down to the trail again.

With a brief look to their left to make sure Tanner wasn't in sight, the boys hurried off in the opposite direction. They rapidly retraced their steps to the point where they expected to find the lava tube through which they'd crawled.

Panting with exertion and anxiety, Josh frowned and looked around. "Hmm, I thought it was right about here."

"It was. But I don't see it. Or maybe we walked past without seeing it. It was a pretty small opening."

"It must still be ahead," Josh said.

Tank glanced around. "Nothing looks familiar. Anyway, we can't stay here debating! The sergeant may realize we fooled him and come this way again!"

"I know, but we can't afford to lose any more time." Josh's voice rose a little in his frustration. "We've got to make a decision, but it'd better be the right one."

"Let's go back and look for the tube opening."

"I don't think it's back that way. Maybe we'd save time if you went back and checked while I go on. We can meet here in a few minutes."

"No, you don't! I'm not taking a chance on getting separated or lost. I'm going where you go."

Josh closed his eyes and said a quick, silent prayer. *Lord, which way? We have to find a way out of here so we can get help for Josh's father, Pua, and her brother.*

Opening his eyes, Josh briefly glanced all around. The ocean lay about 300 yards behind him. He looked back, but there was no sign of the sergeant or the tube. "This way," Josh decided, continuing inland.

"I was afraid you'd say that," Tank said. "I still think it's behind us, but I'm with you."

Josh was reasonably sure they had somehow passed the lava tube. They moved on cautiously. They came to some stunted kiawe trees and small ponds of brackish water. Josh guessed that tidal surges filtered through the porous rock, mixing seawater with fresh rainwater to create a brackish mixture.

"We didn't pass these before," Tank pointed out.

"I know, but that tube's got to be around here somewhere." After a few anxious moments of searching, Josh cried, "There it is!"

The boys eagerly rushed to the opening. Then Josh stopped and shook his head. "This isn't the same one. It's bigger, maybe three feet wide."

"You're right. This is another one. I told you we missed the first... listen!"

Both boys tensed, standing stock still, their heads tilted to hear more of the noise that had caught Tank's attention. After a moment, there came the unmistakable sound of a booted footstep on lava behind them.

"He's closing in fast!" Tank cried hoarsely.

Josh whirled around, his eyes darting about for some way of escape. There was nothing except a pile of rocks.

Tank pointed. "What are those? They look out of place along this trail."

Josh frowned, trying to remember something. "I think

that's a kind of trail marker the ancient Hawaiians used. My father told me that anthropologists take aerial photographs of these things. I think he called them rock cairns. They look like bubbles in the photographs."

"Why would anyone take pictures of these things?"

"Because they may indicate there's a burial cave or chamber nearby, usually with a hidden entrance."

"Oh, great! That's what we need—another bunch of bones and skulls! I'm still nervous from being so close to those we found on the ledge."

"They won't hurt us, but the sergeant can," Josh replied. "Come on, we're losing time."

A few steps later, he started to ease past a thorny kiawe tree, then stopped suddenly and peered through the sparse branches. "There's another tube!"

He gently moved some kiawe branches and bent to look inside the entrance, which was about three feet high.

"I can see daylight at the other end," he announced. "It's about 25 feet long. Do you want to crawl back in there and see if we can get away from the sergeant, or stay on this trail and try to outrun him?"

"We're lost," Tank replied glumly. "No matter what we do, we're going to be more lost and lose more time."

"Well, as long as we're still free, we've got a chance of helping your father and the others back at camp. I'm in favor of going through this tube."

"He'll look in it. He'll see us."

"Not if we crawl out the other end."

"We'll still be lost."

"Yes, but we'll still be free. Now, are you coming?"

Tank scowled, glancing first at the tube opening and then back toward where they'd heard the footstep. "Okay," he decided, "I'm with you. But if I ever get out this, I'm never again going near this part of the island!"

The lava tube was very rough, skinning Josh's hands and knees even more than they were before. At the other end, he peered out. It dropped off onto a short ledge.

There the boys stood upright and looked around. Both ends of the ledge ended against steep cliffs, yet there was another, even larger lava-tube entrance.

"Unless we go back," Josh explained, "our only other choice is to crawl into this tube and see where it goes."

"Probably to another burial place," Tank said miserably.

Josh quickly peered into the entrance, which was about four feet wide. The interior was so dark that Josh couldn't see any light. "I don't see the other end, but there has to be another opening somewhere. I'm going in. You coming?"

He entered on hands and knees with Tank muttering close behind. Josh was surprised to feel dust on his hands and fingers, indicating nothing had disturbed the place for years.

The light fell off rapidly as Josh led the way deeper and deeper into the tube. His breathing seemed ragged and uneven. That was magnified by the enclosed space so that the sound bounced off the tube and echoed strangely. To Josh, it sounded almost as though he were listening to someone—or something—else breathing.

We can't go back! he told himself, struggling with his fear. *The sergeant would probably be close enough that we'd never get away. We've got to keep going.*

"I see something!" He stopped on hands and knees to consider what lay ahead. "It's a little lighter. I think it's the other end of the tube!"

"Well, don't just stay there! Move!"

Moments later, with scratched hands and sore knees, Josh reached the source of light. He was surprised to realize that it wasn't from the other end of the tube. Instead, a shaft of sunlight from directly overhead bored a hole in the gloomy interior.

When Tank breathlessly crawled up beside him, Josh squinted upward. "It's like a blowhole, I think. Only instead of being filled with water that spurts up with the incoming tide, this one's just a plain old opening."

"That sunlight sure looks good!" Tank squirmed to get a better look. "This shaft goes up only about ten feet, so we can climb out easily."

Josh started to get to his feet, then stopped. His eyes strained to make out something in the half-gloom of the tube where it continued. "Can you see it?" he asked in an awed tone.

"See what?"

"The canoe."

"I don't see any canoe."

The interior of the lava tube, partially illuminated by the sunlight spilling in from above, created a weak, reflected glow just ahead of Josh's discerning eyes.

"There," he moved his hand into the shaft of sunshine. "An old Hawaiian canoe about 12 feet long." His finger traced the outline in the air. "See it?"

"No, I don't see... oh yeah! But it's not really a canoe. It's just—dust!"

It was true. The craft had turned to dust, leaving only a perfect outline against the tube wall and floor where it had been left long ago.

Josh's natural curiosity forced him to crawl over for a better look. He was within a few feet when he suddenly sucked in his breath and drew back.

Tank, sitting in the shaft of sunlight, called in a frightened whisper, "What's the matter?"

"Come see for yourself," Josh urged.

"I'm probably going to hate myself," Tank muttered, crawling to Josh. "But I may as well...oh!"

"There are three of them," Josh whispered, pointing. "Buried in full regalia—tapa cloth,* feathered capes, and weapons, along with their canoe. They must have been great warriors."

"One's got some kind of a stone on his chest." Tank's voice was barely audible. "See how bright it is?"

"Yeah! He might have been a chief or someone special. Maybe the other two were his bodyguards. But I wonder how come these aren't just skeletons like the ones we saw on the ledge."

"Maybe being in this lava tube sort of mummified them,"

STRANGE HIDING PLACES 107

Tank guessed. "Maybe the air's so dry that their tapa cloth and feathers didn't turn to dust. But that doesn't explain why the canoe did. Anyway, let's get out of here before we end up like them."

Josh hesitated, staring in wonder at such a rare sight. "The museums would love to know about this. Only I'd want to tell my father first. He could write it up in his newspaper."

"My dad needs us to get out of here!" Tank said firmly. "I'm going. You coming?"

Moments later, the boys sprawled on rough lava beside the shaft. There was no sign of their relentless pursuer. There was nothing but ancient tumbled folds of lava, the typical Hawaiian clouds high overhead, and silence. The stillness was so intense Josh thought he could hear his own heart beating against his eardrums.

"Now what?" Tank asked when he was breathing more regularly. "We're so lost that I'm totally turned around. Which way's the highway?"

Josh studied the sun's position. "It's past noon, so that's west." He pointed left. "We need to go north." He swung his hand around to indicate straight ahead. "Let's climb that little ridge over there. If I'm right, we should see Mauna Loa."

"Since it's more than two miles high, we should see it," Tank joked.

"The volcano must still be erupting," Josh said, walking straight ahead across rough lava that sliced little pieces out of the toes on his boots. "Remember when we smelled the sulphur?"

"That's all we'd need, being lost and blundering into one of those vents. You've seen them on television news. They squirt melted lava high into the air. And one can open up right under your feet."

"Now you're scaring yourself," Josh chided his friend. "Come on! If we see Mauna Loa when we get to the top of that hill, we can eat Pua's food while we walk."

"I've been scared so long and so often I haven't thought about eating. But come to think of it, I'm so empty my belly button's rubbing against my backbone."

Laughing lightly in spite of their circumstances, the boys neared the top of the rise. But even before they reached the peak, the great bulk of Mauna Loa rose up ponderously before them.

"We made it!" Tank cried, thumping Josh on his back. "We're going straight at last. If we just keep moving, we'll find the highway and some help."

Josh nodded, catching his breath. He glanced back and stiffened. "Oh no, I can't believe it!"

In the distance, Sergeant Tanner headed straight across the lava toward the boys.

About 50 yards behind him, trotted Maka, the dog.

Chapter Eleven

SHOWDOWN ON AN OLD LAVA FLOW

Tank groaned in disappointment. "I spoke too soon. I should have known we hadn't made it until we reached the highway and found somebody to help us."

Josh shaded his eyes to study the man and dog heading toward them from the sea. "Maka doesn't look listless now. In fact, there doesn't seem to be anything the matter with him. Hmm, I wonder if the sergeant knows Maka's about 50 yards back of him."

"What difference does it make? We don't want either of them to get close to us. Come on!" Tank turned around and started running up the hill again. "Maybe we'll see the highway when we get to the top. I hope it's close."

Josh's legs began to ache from the fast pace, and his lungs burned as he gasped for air. "Did you notice that the sergeant doesn't have his rifle anymore?"

"He doesn't?" Tank asked in surprise. He twisted his head for a brief glance backward. "You're right. What do you suppose happened to it?"

"Who knows? Maybe he dropped it trying to climb one of those cliffs."

Tank said between panting breaths, "Yeah, and maybe when he dropped the gun, it went off accidentally, and that was the shot we heard."

"Well, there's no use guessing. Save your breath."

The boys slowed as they labored closer to the summit. Josh stole a quick glance over his shoulder. The sergeant was still running, but veering off to the left. Josh frowned. "Wonder why he's going that way?"

Tank looked briefly without slowing. "I don't care where he goes as long as he doesn't follow us."

Josh shook off an uneasy feeling about the sergeant's change of direction. Josh shifted his gaze to the dog. "Look!" he exclaimed, "Maka's not following the sergeant anymore. He's coming straight for us."

For a moment, both boys slowed and studied the strange dog. He was still trotting in a steady pace that had shortened the distance between himself and the boys.

As they continued their climb, Tank commented, "There isn't a rock or anything to defend ourselves, so what'll we do if he catches up to us?"

"Look for a stick or something, but don't fall."

Tank puffed, "You think he's really got rabies?"

"I don't know, but we'd better not let him get close enough to bite. I just wish he was still following the sergeant instead of us."

In spite of the dog gaining on them, the exertion of running uphill forced the friends to slow to a fast walk. Sergeant Tanner had also slowed as he moved within the boys' peripheral vision.

Tank commented, "He must have some reason for heading off on an angle that way instead of staying right behind us. Do you think he's giving up?"

"If he is, why is he still running?"

As the boys neared the top of the ridge, the massive bulk of Mauna Loa rose in the distance. The peak was hidden by puffy, white clouds.

"I just thought of something," Josh panted, shooting a look toward the sergeant. He was walking now, a little below the boys but also approaching the top of the ridge.
"What if the highway's over where he's heading?"

"I sure hope it's not!" Tank said fervently.

Josh's heart drummed rapidly against his rib cage when he struggled to the crest. He glanced back and caught his breath. "The dog's gone!"

"What?" Tank also looked back. "Where'd he go?"

"There's a little gully." Josh pointed. "Maybe he's down in there."

"At least he's not right behind us anymore. Anyway, my lungs are about to burst. Let's catch our breath and see if we can spot the highway and maybe some cars."

Josh agreed, cautioning Tank to keep a lookout for Maka. The boys stopped, their breathing loud in the desolate silence.

Ahead of them, the beauty and grandeur of Mauna Loa was offset in a single glance. Far down its slope, much closer to the boys, an oozing red-black ribbon of lava flowed from the volcanic eruption. Barely a hundred yards from its source, the magma divided into two streams.

The one on the right was only about 30 feet across. It flowed like a red-hot, thick liquid, toward the ocean, moving faster downhill than a man could run.

The river of melted rock on the left had spread out so that it was about a hundred feet across. It crawled slowly over a previous lava flow that had hardened on the more gradual slope toward the ocean.

"The volcano's still erupting," Tank panted. "But it's not shooting up in big fountains as it was when we flew over it with my dad."

"Maybe the eruption's about to stop. Anyway, the lava's moved a lot farther down the mountain since then." Josh paused, his eyes skimming the area between their ridge and the eruption. "You see the highway?"

"No, but it's got to be down there somewhere."

Josh shaded his eyes and made a hurried panoramic sweep of the whole vast area in front of them. There was no sign of a road or cars, no comforting evidence of houses or people on the ground.

The sound of aircraft drew Josh's attention skyward. A two-engine fixed-wing airplane and two helicopters, like miniature toys, circled above the volcano. That was what

Josh, Tank, and Mr. Catlett had been doing when their engine failed.

"Malihinis* out sightseeing," Josh commented. "I guess Hawaii's the only place in the world where people go to watch an erupting volcano up close instead of getting as far away from it as possible."

"If they weren't so far away, we might be able to signal them to help us." Tank paused, then shook his head. "No, they'd probably think we were just more tourists waving greetings to them."

As Josh agreed, he let his gaze drop down again. He saw only an empty desolation with two dominant features: the mighty mountain in the distance and the fiery eruption closer in with the twin rivers of lava flowing downhill. Just in front of the boys, everything was solid black from an old lava flow.

It resembled cake batter that had frozen into eternal folds of black stone. All of it was very rough. Much of it was nearly flat, although some of the surface was pocked with small crevices and holes from inches to several feet deep. A slip would result in at least nicks and cuts on hands thrust out to break a fall. Stepping into one of the depressions could mean a twisted ankle or more serious injury.

"You sure about the road?" Tank asked anxiously, still gasping for breath. "We were so lost back there that we could be almost anywhere."

"We know about where we are because of the volcano," Josh said with assurance. He turned to check on Sergeant

Tanner, who continued walking, slanting away to the left.
Josh glanced around for Maka. "Still no sign of the dog, but
we'd better get moving again before he sneaks up on us."

As the boys started down the ridge, Josh suddenly stopped with a chilling thought. "Now I know why the sergeant's
going that way!" Josh pointed toward the eruption. "See those
two streams of lava? They look like the ends of an upside-
down letter U."

"Yeah, the one on the right has already reached the
ocean."

That was evident by burning palm trees at the shoreline
and rising masses of steam where the hot lava plunged into
the cool ocean.

Josh shifted his gaze to the left, causing Tank's eyes to
follow. There, like some monstrous snake, the probing head
of the mindless mass twisted and turned ever so slowly, yet
maintained a seaward direction.

"It's going to cut us off!" Tank exclaimed.

"Actually, the sergeant's going to get in between that lava
quadrant's flow, then wait for us because we have to go that
way. It's the only way out. We can't go to the right, because
that lava has already reached the ocean. We can't go straight
because of the volcano."

Tank blurted, "We could go back the way we came."
Then he shook his head. "No, we can't. My dad needs help
fast, so we don't dare go back."

"We could try to get back to the sea where search planes

or boats could see us. No, that won't work, either. Maka's somewhere between us and there."

Their desperate situation struck both boys hard, forcing them into stunned silence.

Finally Tank asked in a low voice, "What'll we do?"

Josh thought fast. "Since the sergeant doesn't have his gun, the only way he can stop us is with his bare hands. He can't do that if we split up."

"And he'd have to catch us first! So you go around him one way, and I'll go the other. He can't chase us both at once. When he takes out after one of us, the other will get away and find help for my father."

"I think that'll work." Josh swept the area behind them. "I'd feel better if I knew where that dog went."

"Me too. Hey, did you see that?"

"See what?"

"A flash of light over the ocean." Tank shaded his eyes and stared in that direction. "There it is again! It's sunlight reflecting off an airplane or helicopter. Maybe it's the Coast Guard or Civil Air Patrol."

Both boys strained to see against the glare of the huge expanse of empty, slate-gray ocean. The sun's rays flashed again, then twice more in rapid succession.

"There!" Josh pointed. "Light airplanes! See them? They're searching for us. But we're too far away. They'll never see us."

"They must not have spotted the wreckage of our plane

yet. Otherwise, they wouldn't be working so far offshore. But maybe they'll come this way."

Tank continued, "My father told me that search planes fly in quadrants or grids. Different groups fly different search quadrants. He said that sometimes a couple of helicopters will help, but they fly the opposite route from what the fixed-wing planes took. Maybe those planes out there will see our wreckage when they switch grids and fly closer to shore."

"That's possible," Josh admitted. "The water's so clear that they'll see our plane, just as we saw those old shipwrecks when we were coming down."

"They'll find it." Tank's voice seemed to indicate a confidence he didn't really feel. "Or the Coast Guard helicopter will when it searches this area."

"If we had something shiny like a mirror, even at this distance we might be able to reflect the sun into the cockpit and make one of the pilots see us." Josh glanced down at his meager possessions. All he had was the olive-drab military canteen and the package Pua had given him.

With sudden hope, he reached inside his shirt and removed the package. Hurriedly opening it, he sighed in disappointment. "Nothing but rice wrapped in a ti leaf, and an old military poncho. How about your package?"

Tank's quick examination produced the same items.

Josh shot a longing, hopeful glance toward the ocean. The search planes had moved on. Josh swallowed his disappointment and tried to sound logical.

"Well, even if they had found our plane or that black-sand beach where we swam ashore, they probably would never spot that hole in the cliff leading to the camp. So it's still up to us."

"Think we should eat a little rice?" Tank asked. "I'm starved to death, and the sergeant's not going to do anything until we try getting by him."

"My insides are hollow, but I can run better with an empty stomach. Maybe I'll just drink some water."

"Guess you're right," Tank said.

Both boys sipped from their canteens and replaced them on their belts. They slipped their packages inside their shirts and looked at the sergeant.

He had removed his backpack and stood waiting for them in the distance.

Josh observed, "Well, we have to try getting by him. It's the only way. If he catches me, you keep going. Find help for your father."

"You do the same if he catches me, okay?"

Josh nodded, taking one final look at the dangerous situation. The dog still was nowhere in sight, but the sergeant waited between the lava and the sea. He removed a rope from his backpack and shook out a loop at the end.

"What's that?" Tank asked with a frown. "A lasso?"

"Sure is! He's going to try roping us like cattle. Now, do you want to run to his right or left?"

"Doesn't matter! Let's just do it!"

"I'll go left. Keep away from his rope! Ready? Now!"

The boys split off, putting distance between them but running so that they would pass well to either side of the sergeant. He waited, legs braced, holding the lariat* loosely and watching them.

Will he chase me? Or Tank? Josh wondered as he ran across the old, hardened lava flow. *And where's Maka?*

A quick, probing glance failed to reveal the dog's whereabouts. Josh shifted his gaze toward Tank and the magma flowing toward him. Josh had often seen similar flows on television news.

This slow-moving fork of lava was covered with a rough black crust. It momentarily broke in spots, showing glowing red-hot contents beneath. Josh wasn't too concerned, because Tank could escape its danger on the fairly level ground where he was running.

Josh's thoughts were broken by Tank's distant shout. "Josh! Behind you!"

Josh spun around in sudden terror.

Chapter Twelve

INTO THE VOLCANO

Josh's heart gave a violent leap at the sight of Maka emerging from a small gully 20 feet away. The scrawny black dog panted, his tongue rolling in and out of his open mouth. He looked at Josh with those strange eyes that had given him his Hawaiian name.

Don't run! Josh's mind warned. *Sometimes a dog will attack if you try to run.* Josh tried to say something soothing. *Nice dog!* he thought, but the words wouldn't come. His thudding heart seemed to have stuck in his throat, cutting off all sound. Josh could only manage to move his dry, mute tongue, which made a clicking noise.

With an effort, Josh forced his attention from the menacing dog to glance around for some kind of defensive weapon. There was nothing on the old lava, not even a rock or stick.

Josh turned his eyes back to the dog, keenly aware that the animal might have deadly rabies. *Can't let him bite me!* As a last resort, Josh shifted his weight to his left foot to kick with the heavy right boot while Maka drew nearer.

Except for his loud panting, Maka was silent. He stopped about ten feet from Josh.

"Good dog, Maka," Josh managed to say in a scared croak. The words sounded silly and insincere to Josh, yet he wanted them to be true. He tried again with more conviction and lots of hope. "Good dog!" This time, Josh's voice was steadier, more soothing.

For a long moment, Maka silently stared up at Josh. Then, abruptly, Maka shifted his strange-looking eyes in the direction of the sergeant and Tank.

Josh sighed with relief, then noisily sucked in another breath and held it. The dog broke into a trot, his toenails clicking on the hard, rough lava, heading directly toward the sergeant and Tank. Josh heard Maka growl deep in his throat. Hackles on the back of his neck started to stand erect.

Both Tank and Sergeant Tanner had stopped to watch Josh and Maka. They were in a straight line, with Tank a hundred feet to the man's right.

The sergeant moved first. He took a few fast steps to the dead skeletal branches of a small tree that had been burned in the last lava flow.

What's he doing? Josh asked himself. *He can't hide behind that little tree. There's not enough left to . . .*

Josh interrupted his thought as the sergeant broke off a brittle limb about five feet long. He whirled, gripping the limb as a club to meet the oncoming dog.

Remembering his own terror of moments before, Josh

was tempted to run and help Tanner.

Tank's voice changed Josh's mind. "Now's our chance! Let's run!" Tank followed up his shouted instructions by racing away across the rough, broken old lava flow, leaving the dramatic scene behind.

Josh hesitated, fighting mixed feelings as the dog now circled the man just out of the club's range. He remembered Pua saying the sergeant had kicked Maka. Josh also recalled that his primary mission was to help Tank's father, Pua, and her brother. Fighting guilt for leaving the sergeant to face the dog alone, Josh fled after Tank.

Several minutes later, having come together and passed the slow-moving lava, the boys again turned upslope toward Mauna Loa. Their tortured lungs and aching legs forced them to stop and rest momentarily.

Gasping for air, the boys looked back. The ocean stretched like gray slate toward the horizon, but in circling the river of magma, the boys had topped another small ridge on the great mountain. This blocked the view of where they'd left dog and man facing each other.

Tank finally managed to ask through ragged gasps, "What do you think happened down here?"

"I don't know. I hope the sergeant didn't get bitten, but I also hope he didn't hurt Maka with that club."

"Well, we can't do anything about it, one way or another. We have to find that highway or somebody to help us."

Josh nodded, pivoting to see if there was any sign of the

highway. There wasn't. Disappointed but trying to not be discouraged, Josh lowered his eyes to examine the surrounding terrain.

The old and new lava flows had been left behind. The land was now typical of what the boys had covered on day hikes with their family or friends on ancient Hawaiian trails. The volcanic eruptions that had built the mountain eons ago had slowly turned to dirt. Plants and trees had obtained a hold, sending up leaves and flowers.

"Look at the toes on my boots," Tank grumbled. "That old lava has sliced them to pieces."

Josh lifted his own boots and brushed down the little pieces of leather that had been peeled back. "Mine too." He turned his right ankle over so that he could see the bottom of his ribbed soles. They were also cut and pitted. "I'm sure glad that we didn't have our tennis shoes on when our plane went down."

Tank studied the sky. "Starting to get late. We don't have much time before dark."

"Clouding up too," Josh observed. "I think the way we're heading will take us above where the volcano's erupting. According to the map Pua drew, the highway goes beyond it and right through the Hawaii Volcanoes National Park. So if we keep going up this way, sooner or later, even if we're lost, we have to run across the highway. We'll flag down the first car we see."

"Dark clouds mean it's going to rain hard," Tank commented. "When pretty, white, fluffy clouds drift over, they make only a drizzle."

"That mountain means we have to climb. So we'd better get at it, because sooner or later either the sergeant or the dog is likely to be on our trail again."

The boys started walking, alternating their attention between the rising steepness of the mountain before them and the trail behind them. Josh felt hopeful that if Maka followed, his earlier behavior might mean he would be friendly if he caught up to them.

But we can't depend on that, he cautioned himself, feeling the pull on his legs as the angle of climb increased.

Tank said, "If the sergeant's still after us, he's going to be very mad. What do you think he'll do if he catches us now?"

"Don't think about that. Think about helping your father, Pua, and Keoni. We can't let them down."

"That's right. We don't dare let anyone or anything stop us from getting help back to the camp—soon."

As they climbed higher, searching for some sign of humanity in the late afternoon, the boys were forced to stop and rest more often. On one of those stops, they spotted an ancient Hawaiian trail. It had been beaten down over countless centuries by thousands of bare feet.

"It'll be easier walking on that," Tank said with a grin.

"And faster, too. It'll probably lead us to somebody before nightfall. So maybe now's a good time to eat and have another drink."

After they had finished their meal of rice and sipped

sparingly from their canteens, Tank stood and stared thoughtfully down the way they'd come.

"You know," he said with feeling, "in my whole life, I never really hated anybody."

"Me neither."

"But I could come close to hating that pupule Captain Kidd and Sergeant Tanner."

"Christians aren't supposed to hate. Just love and forgive," Josh said.

"That's easy to say in Sunday school and places like that. Then I think of my father needing medical help, and how those two men are trying to keep us from doing that, and that makes me really mad!"

"I'm feeling something like that myself," Josh admitted. "But I'm also trying to understand those men. They went through terrible things in Vietnam, and sometimes the human mind just can't deal with awful memories."

"My father was there too, but he's dealing with it just fine."

"Maybe the lieutenant and the sergeant went through things in the jungle and on the ground that a helicopter pilot didn't in the sky."

"You making excuses for them?" Tank's voice rose slightly.

"No, I'm just trying to understand, that's all."

Tank said grimly, "If anything happens to my father because of those two, I'll never understand. And I don't think I can ever forgive them, either."

"Don't get yourself all worked up," Josh said soothingly. "Let's go on and try to find that highway while it's still daylight."

The boys resumed their trek as the sun's lower rim touched the distant Pacific horizon. The going was easier on the old Hawaiian trail, so they made good time in spite of the increasingly steep climb up the mountain.

Josh was puffing when he said, "I'm sure glad for these trails. My father said that the old Hawaiians were big people with long strides. They had what he called a barter economy, or trading. That meant that they had to make trails to connect different parts of the island.

"They made trails from inland where the farmers grew taro* and other vegetables to trade with the people who lived by the ocean. Then they traded back and forth."

"They had to be in good shape to climb this trail," Tank said, panting. "We're climbing fast, and I'm feeling it."

The first drops of rain fell at dusk. The boys put on their ponchos while scanning their back trail. Just as Tank announced he didn't see anything, Josh pointed at a movement against the skyline.

"There's the sergeant! He's still hot on our trail."

"I see him. But I don't see the dog, do you?"

"No. I wonder what happened to him?"

"Who knows? I'm just glad we spotted the sergeant before it's too dark to see where we're going."

The boys kept going while the light rain turned into a semitropical downpour. The trail became slick so that even their hiking boots with their ribbed soles were useless. When Josh slipped and started sliding over the side, he was saved only by plowing painfully into two little bushes.

"You okay?" Tank called softly from the trail.

"I think so, but we'd better stop before we have a more serious accident."

"I just hope the sergeant doesn't have a flashlight, so he has to stop too."

The boys found a wide area beside the trail and sat down. They used the long, loose ends of their army ponchos to protect their backsides from the muddy ground.

"Going to be a long, miserable night," Tank muttered, drawing his chin inside the poncho hood.

"It'll be worse if the sergeant has a flashlight and keeps following our trail."

"There you go again, saying cheerful things!"

"Even if the rain washes out our tracks, there's no place to go except this trail. There's certainly no place to hide around here either." Josh squinted around but ducked his head when the rain pelted him. "This is the first wide spot we found on this trail, and you can be sure he'll check that with his light if he has one."

"Let's think of a plan in case he shows up."

"We have to stay on this trail, because it's too dangerous to leave it and either try to climb up or go down this mountain. But even on the trail, we can't outrun the sergeant in the dark. We could slip as I did and go tumbling down..."

Josh broke off as the ground seemed to move below him. It was now too dark to see Tank sitting next to him, but Josh heard his friend leap to his feet.

Josh did the same, standing in uncertainty of what was happening. "You felt that too, huh?"

"What is it? An earthquake?"

"I don't know. It felt like the earthquakes we used to have in Los Angeles. But this was just a little... there it is again! And look over there!"

A couple of hundred yards away, the blackness of the rainy night was suddenly ripped open. A brilliant tongue of flaming liquid leaped skyward.

Instinctively, both boys drew back, covering their eyes with their forearms at the fountain's fiery intensity. It rose 200 to 300 feet in the air before the top started to fall back to earth.

"What is it?" Tank whispered in awe. "Another eruption?"

Josh peered through the pelting rain, now visible against the sudden brightness. In the reflected light, he could make out the top of a cinder cone a few hundred feet tall. The fountain of lava spurted from the cone's peak.

"I think it's what's called 'fountaining,'" Josh replied as another, harder tremor vibrated up his legs. "One of the rifts must have fractured."

"You mean we're almost on top of an erupting volcano?" Tank threw up his arms to keep his balance as the tremors continued. "Hey, I can't stand up!"

Josh grabbed his friend and tried to help both of them keep their feet. "My father wrote about something like this in his newspaper," Josh said, trying to sound calm. "If I remember right, he said these fountains of lava coincide with what the scientists called 'harmonic tremors.'"

"Don't use words I don't know!"

"I mean, I think we're standing on top of the fissure that carries lava from deep in the earth to where it's escaping through that vent!"

Tank's voice threatened to crack with fear. "Are you saying we're having an earthquake *and* a volcanic eruption at the same time?"

Before Josh could answer, Tank spun away from the fiery eruption and started down the mountain trail. "Let's get out of here!"

Josh grabbed Tank's arm to stop him. "The sergeant's down that way!"

"Well, we can't go forward because of that new eruption, and we'll die if we stay here!"

Josh didn't answer, but suddenly sniffed. "You smell something burning?" he asked abruptly.

"Yeah, it smells like...Hey, my feet are getting hot!" Tank hastily lifted his right foot.

By the light of the fountain of fire, Josh glimpsed a wisp of smoke arising from Tank's boot. With his right hand, Tank hurriedly reached down and touched the sole.

"It's my boot!" he cried, jerking his hand back. "My boot's on fire!"

Chapter Thirteen

STRANGE HIDING PLACES

T ank put his foot down hard and began stamping wildly. "My boot's on fire! My boot's on fire!"

"Mine too!" Josh exclaimed upon seeing smoke starting to curl up over his feet. "The ground's hot from the lava flowing under it."

The boys had no choice but to retreat. Even if the sergeant was waiting for them on the trail, they rushed down it. Stamping and scrubbing their boots in the muddy trail, they sought to escape the immediate danger.

"Don't fall!" Josh cautioned, leading the way by the reflected light of the column of glowing magma. "If our hands touch this ground, or we slide over the edge. . ."

"Don't say it!" Tank interrupted. "I'm already scared enough without thinking about that."

The drenching rain had muddied the trail so that it was slick as a ti-leaf slide. The boys were forced to go slowly, slipping, sliding, and throwing their arms out to maintain balance.

They went back the way they'd come to where they could

no longer see their way. Josh stopped and quickly stooped to check his boots. "I think the soles are just melted a little," he decided.

"Mine too," Tank said after finishing his examination. "Boy, who would've guessed the ground could get that hot?"

"I sure wouldn't. But I think it's okay now. We're about a hundred yards away from the fountain and not directly over that underground flow of lava anymore."

"Then how come I can still feel those vibrations?"

"The harmonic tremors probably will continue as long as the eruption lasts."

"How long will that be?"

Josh shrugged. "If I were a volcanologist,* maybe I could tell you. But I've heard that these fountains can last from a few hours up to days."

"But we need to get by that eruption to find the highway and send help to my father!"

"I know, but we've probably climbed a couple thousand feet up this mountain. We can't risk leaving the trail in the rain and darkness without a flashlight. We could get seriously hurt, or even killed."

"But I don't want to just sit here, waiting for the sergeant to catch us! The rain's making so much noise against my poncho that I wouldn't hear him until he was right on top of us."

Josh momentarily focused on just how loud the semitropical downpour was on the poncho's hood. He stood uncertainly, trying to think what to do. He squinted down the dark trail to where their pursuer had to come, then back to the erupting pillar of flame.

Tank groaned. "The worst part of all is that we're losing valuable time! Ever since we left camp, we've been delayed by something. Now we're both lost and trapped. So what're we going to do?"

"I don't think we have any other choice but to stay here until daylight. Then we can see to climb around the fountain and keep going until we find somebody."

"What'll we do if the sergeant shows up tonight?"

"The trail's not wide enough for us to split up and go around him as we did before. All we could do is try to stay out of his reach."

"Yeah? How? Remember, he's got a lasso. Hey, how about if we both try to tackle him?"

"We'd probably all roll down the mountain to our deaths. I think the best thing is to split up and hope one of us gets away in the darkness. In the morning, that person would keep looking for help."

"What happens if one of us gets caught?"

"I don't want to think about that. So let's watch out for the sergeant—and Maka—and pray."

"I've been praying my head off. Silent prayers for my dad, for us and Pua and Keoni, for our families in Honolulu. They must think that my dad, you, and I are dead."

"I know. I've tried not to think too much about it because it'd drive me crazy. So I try to fill my mind with other thoughts."

"Such as?"

"Well, I always get comfort from remembering a verse that we learned in Sunday school. You know, the one about trusting in the Lord and not depending on your own understanding. Just acknowledge Him, and He'll direct your paths."*

"It's easy to say and believe that when things are going great, but right now, it's really hard."

"You've got to try."

"I know, but it all looks so hopeless. Everything is against us. And while we sit here, my father could be getting worse and worse."

Josh put his arm around his friend's shoulder, causing the ponchos to make loud rustling sounds. "We're still alive and we're still free," he said comfortingly. "So things certainly could be a lot worse."

Tank said with sudden warmth, "I hate it when you always seem to find a ray of sunshine when it's midnight in a long railroad tunnel and a train's coming!"

Josh chuckled good-naturedly, patted his friend on the back and pulled his hand back under the poncho. "It isn't that I don't see the problems, Tank," he explained soberly. "I know them all too well, and I get scared, but then I always have my faith to hang on to."

"I believe the same as you do," Tank protested.

"I know, but our personalities are different. You're cautious, but I'm always going ahead and doing something. Lots of times it gets me in trouble."

"Gets *us* in trouble is more like it."

"Well, we always get out of it, don't we?"

"So far," Tank admitted glumly. "But if we get out of this one, I think maybe I'll trade you in for a friend who's more like me."

"You wouldn't like him as much as me," Josh kidded.

Both boys fell silent. Josh's mind flashed back to the verse about trust. *Trust in the Lord, not in yourself. Oh sure, I have to do what I can, but trust in Him to direct us. That's God's own promise.**

Josh's thoughts skipped to his grandmother. *What is it she's always saying about promises? "Plead the promises and meet the conditions." Grandma says most people only plead the promises and forget that all biblical promises are conditional. Well, Tank and I are doing our part, so far as we can. So now—trust!*

Josh started to feel better. Comforted, he slowly became aware of the surrounding sounds. The rain still drummed loudly against his poncho hood. The ground rumbled with the magma surging up from somewhere deep in the earth to explode into the air. The noise beat against the boy's ears, yet there were other sounds too. Josh tried to sort them out.

First, there seemed to be a faint moaning from the ground itself. Then there was the violent rush of magma as it spurted above the cinder cone a hundred yards away. The cascading column of melted rock gushed noisily upward for perhaps a thousand feet. Then it fell to earth again with a splattering sound. The cycle never seemed to end, but repeated itself as the night dragged on.

It's scary! But it's wonderful at the same time, Josh thought. He felt so small and insignificant, so totally and utterly tiny and powerless against the awesome spectacle before him.

The fascination began to engulf him. *This is a real once-in-a-lifetime experience. Not many people will ever see or feel or hear anything like this. Yet, somehow, I'm not as scared as I was.*

Josh turned to share that thought with Tank, but saw that his friend's eyes were closed. Josh was unsure if Tank was sleeping, or just blotting out the visual spectacle before them. He decided not to disturb him. Josh shifted his attention from hearing to other senses. His nose occasionally caught the faint stench of sulphur. Since the wind blew from him to the eruption, he felt no danger from potentially deadly vapors.

He seemed to taste something, but couldn't isolate what his tongue found somewhat unpleasant.

His hands weren't touching the ground, yet Josh felt the whole earth trembling. It transferred itself from his seat through his entire body so that he felt as though he were having a never-ending shiver.

The eruption's colors drew his eyes to the source. The magma left its original home deep within the earth by leaping into view as a bright yellow column. The column, now about 30 feet around, soared upward, changing visually along the way. About a third of the way up, the fiery liquid started to take on a faint orange tint.

As it passed the halfway mark into the night sky, the lava began to turn red. A thousand feet above the top of the 600-foot cinder cone, the lava, already cooling, became a brilliant orange.

Then, its upward energy spent in springing to life, the magma fell back to earth in splattering hues. The lava formed a stream running from the cinder cone down the great mountain's side into the rainy blackness of the night.

Here the colors changed again. The thick river of melted stone glowed red as it began its mindless way into the darkness. Josh saw the familiar black crust start to form so that the red-hot interior only momentarily broke through. Yet there was such intense heat that the lava's width could be marked as it yielded to gravity.

Occasionally, a bubble on the stream's surface burst like a red-eyed wink, then disappeared into the black-encrusted river of living rock. In the distance, the lava slowed to almost a crawl. Yet the glowing outline showed the mass was still seeking the shore. There it would create new land for the Big Island.

There's good coming out of this volcano, Josh told himself. *That's strange.* He closed his eyes to mull over that thought while the rain battered his poncho.

He wasn't aware that he'd dozed. One moment, he was turning words over in his mind. The next, he realized he had been asleep. *How long?* he wondered, turning to see if Tank was awake.

He was gone!

Josh leaped to his feet, throwing the poncho's loose covering back so he could get his arms free. One glance showed him that the brilliant fountaining continued, but Tank wasn't between Josh and the eruption.

He whirled around and squinted down the trail to where shadows blocked his vision. The rain had stopped, but light from the fiery pillar reflected off nearby muddy puddles. Josh frowned, aware of something different from what he'd seen earlier.

He took a couple of quick steps, bent, and examined the puddles. *Boot tracks! Two sets. One big, one smaller.* Josh bounced to his feet again. *The sergeant's got Tank!*

Recklessly, Josh plunged down the trail, following the wet footprints. After only a few steps he stumbled over something and fell headlong. Frantically, he started to push himself up with muddy hands.

He got to his knees before something whistled over his head and settled about his arms and chest. *Lasso!* he thought as the rope was jerked tight. His arms were pinned against his chest. With no way to brace himself, he fell face down in the mud.

Then he heard the sergeant's cry of triumph!

Chapter Fourteen

WHEN ALL SEEMS LOST

Spitting muddy water, Josh jerked his face from the trail. He struggled to get to his knees, but Sergeant Tanner leaped astride Josh's back.

"Oh no, you don't!" the man cried, rapidly pulling Josh's hands behind his back. "You just hold still until I get you tied up nice and neat, like your friend!"

Moments later, with soft, cotton rope binding his wrists, Josh was helped to a sitting position in the muddy trail beside Tank. Light from the reflected eruption showed he was similarly bound.

"There!" Tanner exclaimed. "That should hold you until daylight when we can head back to camp." He removed the rough lasso loop from around Josh's shoulders. "Guess I haven't forgotten how to throw a lariat, even though it's been a while since I last tried it."

Josh looked at Tank with concern. "You okay?"

He nodded. "I think so. But I'm sick inside at what's going to happen to my father now."

"Things will work out." Josh tried to sound more confident than he felt. "Remember to trust."

Tank's eyes blazed in the reflected light from the eruption. "Trust? After what's happened?" He shook his head and added bitterly, "All I'm remembering is what these men are doing to my dad!"

Josh lowered his face and lifted his shoulder to try brushing off the mud, but the wet poncho made it worse. Resignedly, Josh focused instead on what his and Tank's capture meant to their original mission.

"I'm sorry, Tank," he said. "If I hadn't dozed off, we wouldn't be tied up like this."

"Don't blame yourself. I fell asleep too. I guess the rain was making so much noise against my poncho that I didn't hear him at all. The first thing I knew, he had his hand over my mouth. He made me walk down the trail to here, where he tied me up. Then he got his lasso out of his pack, plus another short piece of rope, and went back for you."

The sergeant said cheerfully, "I used the little piece to stretch across the trail, like a tripwire in the jungle."

Tanner's voice hardened. "Did you think a couple of kids like you could really escape from me? I survived two tours of duty in the jungles of Vietnam, where a mistake could get you killed. You boys didn't stand a chance."

Josh didn't want to ask, yet he had to know. "What's going to happen to us, Sergeant Tanner?"

"It depends on whether Lieutenant Ross Beacher or

Captain Kidd sits in judgment on you boys."

"He's one and the same person!" Tank snapped.

His captor nodded. "In body, yes, but not in mind. The lieutenant is more tolerant than the captain and might go easy on you. But Captain Kidd might just take the boat out to where the sharks are, tie your hands behind your backs, and make you walk the plank."

"You're kidding!" Josh exclaimed.

"Wish I were," Sergeant Tanner replied with a tone of sincerity. "But the captain's like that."

"That's murder!" Josh cried, struggling to get to his feet in spite of his bound arms. "And if Tank's father dies because you guys wouldn't let us get help for him, that'll be another murder!"

The sergeant shrugged. "Nobody will ever know what happened out here. Besides, I'm a soldier. I obey orders. Now, you two had better try to get some sleep. At daybreak we'll head back for camp."

The next morning Josh's eyes felt heavy from lack of sleep. The awful realization of what their capture meant weighed heavily on his mind.

The sergeant untied the boys' hands so they could use them in coming down the volcanic mountain. However, he looped one end of his lasso around Josh's waist and the other around Tank's.

Tanner explained, "This will keep you from splitting up and running away from me as you did yesterday."

They started down the slippery mountain trail, with Josh ahead of Tank and the sergeant following both.

Hearing Tank moan softly, Josh twisted his head to look back. "What's the matter?"

"This is the most terrible mess we've ever been in!"

Josh forced himself to sound confident. "We've gone through worse times together, and we'll get out of this."

"But now it's not just you and me. It's my dad."

And Pua, Josh added silently. Aloud, he said, "I'm still trusting and trying to think of something that'll get us out of this. So don't give up hope."

The boys, followed by Tanner, walked in silence until they left the mountain and started back over the vast expanse of old lava they had fled across yesterday.

Josh turned to look back at the sergeant. "What'd you do to the dog?"

"When I swung at him with a stick a few times, he gave up and ran off."

"Which way?" Josh wanted to know.

"Back into the jungle." The sergeant motioned in the direction they were heading.

"What if he's really got rabies?" Josh asked with alarm. "He could spread it all through the island."

"Neither Ross nor I believe he's got rabies."

Josh asked, "What if you're wrong?"

Tanner only shrugged and urged the boys forward.

Josh's tiredness and discouragement receded slightly

when they entered the canopy of trees. Josh watched tensely, hoping the dog didn't leap from the underbrush.

At the first running stream, Josh was allowed to wash the mud off his hands and face.

Tank also refreshed himself in the water. His face was set in hard lines, and he muttered darkly to himself. "I hope there's a chance to get even with these two men for what they're doing to my dad!" he growled, scowling at the sergeant. "I hate those two!"

"Being bitter won't help," Josh cautioned.

"It's not *your* father who's going to die because of what these bush vets are doing!"

Josh sighed softly. "I haven't given up hope, and neither should you. Maybe I can learn something from the sergeant that'll help us when we see the lieutenant."

"Nothing'll help if he's acting like that pupule Captain Kidd again!"

Josh realized that nothing he could say now would change Tank's mind.

He turned to the sergeant walking behind him. "Why do you stay with the lieutenant when he can switch in seconds from being a nice person to that weird pirate?"

"If somebody twice saved your life, as Ross did mine in 'Nam, you'd do the same as I'm doing now."

Josh nodded with understanding. He could imagine the invisible bond that held the two bush vets together. Yet the boy didn't comprehend the strange mental quirks that made the lieutenant change in seconds from a nice person to the brutal pirate, Captain Kidd.

Josh asked the sergeant, "Why does he switch back and forth from one personality to another?"

"How should I know?"

Josh persisted. "You must have some idea about why he sometimes thinks he's a pirate, don't you?"

Tanner didn't answer for a moment. Finally he said, "Well, yes, I've thought a lot about it, and I've come up with a theory. You see, Ross was too nice a man to have to fight in the jungles of 'Nam.

"He was also just a kid who'd never seen a dead person until he got there. I went with him on his first patrol, and we were ambushed. Lost several men. Well, that hit Ross hard, but the war went on, and he seemed to adjust well enough to do what had to be done. I was with him all through that mess. We came home together."

"You were with him after the war too?"

"For awhile. Officers and enlisted men aren't supposed to fraternize, but after what Ross and I had been through, we didn't care about military protocol anymore. So we came home as American soldiers have done since George Washington's day. But nobody on the Mainland understood us. It seemed that they didn't want to understand.

"For the first time in history, our country was divided. Our own people didn't give us parades and make nice speeches about us as they had in all our country's previous wars. Instead, we were treated like dirt, like we were responsible for the Vietnam war."

Tanner spat contemptuously as though expelling some bad taste from his mouth. "Enough talk," he said firmly.

As they continued working their way through the Hawaiian jungle toward the camp where the boys had fled the day before, Josh's curiosity bubbled over. He kept walking but raised his voice so the sergeant behind him could hear.

"When did the lieutenant get married and have Pua and Keoni?"

For a moment, the sergeant didn't answer. Then he said quietly, "Ross met Lilia* while stationed in Hawaii before shipping out to 'Nam. After the war, he called her long distance from the Mainland, then flew over here. They eventually got married and moved to Los Angeles.They had Pua and Keoni, but gradually the pressures of civilization and the antagonism toward us vets continued to bother Ross.

"The jungle seemed to call to him, and Lilia said she understood that. She urged him to try the jungles here in Hawaii. So he brought his family back to Honolulu, then left them. Because I was also fed up with civilization and the way people treated us vets, I went with him. At first, we grew marijuana only for our own use. Later, we expanded into selling it. Recently, we started smuggling exotic birds and animals to sell."

When the sergeant lapsed into silence, Josh asked, "Did everything go along okay until the lieutenant learned his wife had died?"

The sergeant said. "He'd always felt a lot of guilt about leaving them. Lilia had said she understood, but Ross thought his kids never would. He said they'd feel abandoned, so he went back for them. But their coming changed things. Nothing's been quite the same with the kids here."

"Did the lieutenant ever act like a pirate before his children came here?" Josh asked.

"Oh, yes. He had always read about pirates the way some men follow sports. But Ross got much worse after the kids arrived." The sergeant paused, then added, "That's enough questions. Let's head on back to camp."

Josh looked at Tank and swallowed hard at the strange look on his friend's face.

"What's the matter?" Josh whispered.

"They can't do this to us and my dad!" Tank grated between clenched teeth. "I'm going to get even with them!"

"You saw what bitterness did to the lieutenant. Don't let it happen to you!"

"You keep talking to the sergeant," Tank said sourly. "I'm thinking how to escape from these men!"

"I'm trying to think of a way out too. The more we know about them, the better chance we'll have."

Tank grunted in apparent disagreement and lapsed into silence as he walked along.

Hurt by his friend's rebuff, Josh nevertheless continued seeking information from the sergeant. "You didn't finish telling me about the theory you have on why the lieutenant sometimes thinks he's a pirate."

"I think I've said enough," the sergeant replied.

Josh decided to keep trying. "Why do you think he imagines he's a pirate instead of someone else?"

Sergeant Tanner hesitated before answering. "Maybe because old-time captains were called masters in those days, and they were the absolute authority on board ship. The master answered to no one. This was especially true of a pirate vessel. The master could be cruel and heartless, doing what he thought was right, including passing judgment in life and death matters.

"So I think that maybe when things get too hard for Lieutenant Beacher, he becomes Captain Kidd. As master of a pirate ship, he could make tough decisions without losing any sleep over them."

Josh thought that made sense as they made their way past the cages of squawking birds and mewing cats. The snake's cage was closed, but Maka's still stood open. Josh glanced hastily around, half-fearing he'd see the dog, but Maka wasn't in sight.

Tank whispered, "I've got to see my dad!"

"I'll see if I can do something to keep their attention so you can slip away and check on him," Josh replied in a low voice.

There was no chance to do that before the sergeant herded the boys toward the table in the clearing under the trees.

Josh's heart sank at sight of the lieutenant dressed as Captain Kidd.

He looked up from where he was pouring some kind of oily substance from a leather bucket onto his hands. "So, Mr. Hook!" he roared, "You're back with the mutineers, eh? Bring them here! Then assemble the ship's company so all may see how Captain Kidd punishes those who disobey."

Josh gulped audibly, trying to swallow a lump of fear in his throat as Tanner removed the rope from Tank and himself. "Sir, if you'll just listen ..."

"Silence!" the pirate roared.

Tank protested, "Please let me see my father..."

"I said, 'Silence!'" Captain Kidd slammed the oil container down on the table so hard some of its contents splashed over the top. "First, ye'll have a fair trial. Then ye'll both walk the plank!"

Tank's anguished groan was matched by Josh's own sickening sensation of total defeat.

"Daddy!" Keoni's frightened voice jerked everyone's head around. The boy dashed wildly into camp. "Daddy, come quick! Pua's caught in the Toilet Bowl, and she's drowning!"

Chapter Fifteen

A FINAL DESPERATE EFFORT

Keoni darted past Josh, Tank, and Sergeant Tanner to his father. "Pua's drowning, Daddy!" the boy shouted, gesturing frantically. "She got caught when the water was draining out of the Toilet Bowl. Her legs are stuck in the tube. I tried to get her out, but the water came back. She held her breath, only she'll drown if we don't get her out fast. Come on! Run, Daddy!"

Keoni's father, dressed as the pirate captain, stared wordlessly down at the boy.

Josh whirled to face the sergeant. "I was afraid somebody would get trapped like that someday. Let me have your rope. We're going to need it."

"Daddy!" Keoni pleaded, grabbing his father's hands. "Don't stand there! Come save her. She can't hold her breath forever."

Hastily grabbing the lasso from Tanner's outstretched hands, Josh glanced at the man in pirate's costume. He had not moved although Keoni tugged frantically at his hands.

The father stared down at his boy without seeming to recognize or understand him.

"Keoni, he thinks he's Captain Kidd!" Josh exclaimed, hurriedly slipping the coiled lasso over his left shoulder. "He probably doesn't recognize you." Josh whirled toward Tank. "You go check on your father." Josh spun around to face the sergeant. "Grab that bucket of oil! Let's go help Pua!"

Without waiting for anyone to reply, Josh broke into a frantic run across the clearing. He heard Sergeant Tanner pounding after him.

O Lord! Josh prayed silently but fervently. *O Lord, don't let us be too late!*

Tanner, carrying the bucket of oil, outran Josh, passing him as they left the jungle and entered the narrow volcanic trail beside the ocean. Josh saw the sergeant reach the Toilet Bowl, set the oil container at the rim, and jump into the pit, fully dressed.

When Josh arrived moments later, panting hard from all-out running, his galloping heart seemed to stop at the terrible sight below.

The water level dropped fast, carrying Tanner down with it. Josh could see Pua on the very bottom of the pit, under water. She lay on her back, her body up to the waist out of sight in the lava tube that led to the sea. Her long brown hair floated about her face, covering it.

Is she dead? The fearful question seared Josh's mind as he gripped the lasso and jumped after the sergeant.

The water had already fallen about ten feet when Josh landed with a mighty splash beside Tanner.

"If she didn't panic," the sergeant cried, his voice echoing strangely against the volcanic rock sides of the pit, "she might have been able to hold her breath until the water drained out. Then she could breathe until it comes in again. It's only a 30- or 40-second cycle."

Josh nodded in understanding, watching in fearful fascination as the force of the outgoing current sucked Pua's long hair across her face and upper body. "She's not moving!" Josh shouted, hearing his words bounce back from the walls now far out of reach above.

"Maybe she's saving her energy."

The sergeant, having longer legs than the boy, touched bottom first. He instantly bent and grabbed the girl's head, lifting it above the last of the draining water gurgling noisily out the tube.

Pua explosively exhaled and breathed in with sobbing gulps.

"She's alive!" Josh yelled with sudden joy.

"Get me out!" Pua managed to gasp, gripping both the sergeant's hands and straining to free her trapped legs."Oh, please! Please get me out!"

"We will!" Josh promised, dropping the rope onto the few inches of water remaining on the bottom.

Tanner ordered, "Grab her hands and pull when I tell you. I'll reach under her armpits. Ready?"

When Josh nodded, still panting hard from his run, the

man yelled, "Now!"

Josh braced his heavy boots on the bottom of the wet pit as best he could and leaned backward, pulling on Pua's wrists with all his strength.

The sergeant, squatting in the water with both hands under the girl's armpits, pulled so hard that the cords and blood vessels in his neck stood out sharply.

Pua screamed, but Josh knew that she would have to bear the pain to live. He kept pulling, trying to keep his balance on the pit's slippery floor.

When Pua shrieked again, the sergeant eased off. "Let go, Josh!" he commanded. "We're hurting her."

Josh obeyed, snatching up the rope in one fast motion. "Drop this loop around her! Maybe that'll work."

When Pua's hands were released, she thrust them into the small amount of standing water and started clawing wildly at the pit's floor, trying to drag herself free. "Get me out! Get me out, please!" she pleaded between very fast, deep breaths.

"Calm down!" the sergeant ordered, slipping the lasso loop over her head and pulling it taut under her armpits. "You're hyperventilating!* If you keep that up, you won't be able to hold your breath if the water comes in again before we get you out of here!"

"I'll try," Pua sobbed weakly. "But I can't hold on much longer!"

The sergeant handed Josh the rope's loose end. "Back up with this as far as you can. Keep it low and straight. We'll pull together on my order."

Josh ran, splashing water, until he reached the pit's other wall. "Hurry!" he urged. "I can hear the water starting back in!"

"Now! Pull, Josh, pull!"

Josh reached out as far as he could and gripped the rope with one hand in front of the other. He tugged mightily, rearing back and pulling straight. The rope leaped from the water, throwing big droplets.

The incoming water exploded through the lava tube and past Pua's trapped lower body. It struck her full in the face. Josh heard her gasp as the stream's power hit her. He wondered if she'd managed to take a deep breath before the water flooded over her.

The pit filled so rapidly that the rising water lifted Josh and the sergeant upward. For a moment, Josh debated what to do about the rope. He thought of dropping it, but changed his mind and held on to it.

"Get the oil!" he yelled. "I'll stay with her."

Josh took a deep breath and forced himself down under the swirling, churning water, using the rope to offset the buoyancy of his body. He saw the man's feet pass overhead, out of sight.

Josh fought against the power of the incoming current to grab Pua's hands. Her eyes were open and wide with fright as she held her breath and desperately clung to him. He squeezed her hands, over and over, trying to comfort and reassure her as the seconds passed. He began to feel an urgent need to breathe.

Every part of his mind shrieked for him to let go and rise to the surface to breathe, but he fought off that desperate feeling. *If I do that, she may give up and take a breath! If she does, she'll choke and drown.*

A tremendous sense of relief swept over Josh when the rush of water from the tube slowed, then stopped. Precious seconds passed before Josh felt the water start draining out. He glanced up as the sergeant jumped back in to ride the receding water down, holding the bucket.

Josh felt a little lightheaded before the water drained past his nose and mouth and he could breathe. By then, the sergeant was beside him. In another few seconds, Pua's face broke the surface. She gulped hungrily for air, and gagged on a mouthful of saltwater.

Josh exclaimed, "Sergeant, dump the oil over her! Pua, listen to me! Take your hands and smear the oil down your legs as far as you can reach!"

When Josh's instructions were carried out, he again seized the rope and started backing up. The sergeant waded noisily through the last of the standing water, letting the rope slip through his fingers.

Tanner dropped his voice. "This may be our last chance! She's been holding her breath off and on since her brother ran to get us, and she's wearing out!"

Josh nodded, flexing his fingers on the wet rope for a better grip. *Please, Lord!* That was all he said, but it was a prayer straight from his heart.

"Now, Josh!"

Once again, the desperate boy pulled mightily on the rope. His arm muscles started to quiver with the effort. *Nothing's happening! She's still stuck, and the water's covering her again!*

As the pit started refilling, someone jumped in beside Josh. Big hands brushed by Josh's own and settled about the rope between him and the sergeant.

Pua's father! The realization made Josh's hopes spiral upward. *He's pulling too! Where's Keoni? The lieutenant's straining so hard he's going to...Hey! Something's happening!*

The rope suddenly went slack. *She's free!* Josh wanted to shout with joy but the incoming water climbed past his mouth. He kept his eyes open, seeing Pua's father drop the slack rope.

The lieutenant forced his body down against the incoming current from the lava tube until he swept his daughter into his arms. Her lower body and legs were badly cut and bleeding freely, but she was alive.

Her father kicked powerfully, shooting past Josh and the sergeant, carrying Pua upward to life-giving air.

Moments later, panting with exertion beside the sergeant, Josh gripped the rim as the Toilet Bowl completed its cycle of filling the hole.

One glance showed Josh the lieutenant gently laying his daughter on the rough but safe lava. Pua coughed and gasped for air while her father knelt and quickly checked her wounds. Keoni dropped to his knees beside them, crying loudly.

"Whooeee!" Josh cried, thumping the sergeant on the back. "That was something!"

"Sure was," Tanner agreed, looking at Pua and her father. "But we'd never have made it without his help."

Josh sobered, noticing that the lieutenant again was shirtless, clad only in casual shorts. There was no hint of the pirate captain's costume, no sign of the peg leg. The father gathered Pua to his chest, rocking gently and whispering soothing words.

"Josh! Josh!" Tank's cry jerked Josh's head around. His friend was running along the narrow path followed by Keoni. "Is Pua okay?"

"She's got some bad cuts, but she's alive. What about your father?"

"His fever's worse! If we don't get help..."

He broke off suddenly, looking skyward over the ocean. "Helicopter! Josh, it's a helicopter!"

Josh followed Tank's example in looking up, following the beating sound of a chopper. The sun reflected off the white aircraft with the familiar bright orange stripe. Josh yelled, "It's the Coast Guard!"

He almost threw himself out of the pit as the water started going down again. He leaped to his feet and started to wave at the helicopter flying parallel to them, about to pass offshore. Then Josh glanced at his captor.

The lieutenant struggled to his feet, still holding his daughter in his left arm. For a moment, he hesitated, looking down at her bleeding wounds. Then, as if making a decision, he looked up purposefully toward the helicopter.

"Over here!" he shouted, motioning with his right arm toward the low-flying aircraft. "They're over here!"

The chopper banked sharply and headed straight for the people on the shore.

Josh looked beyond the approaching aircraft. *Thank You, Lord! Thank You!*

The helicopter slowed, then hovered directly above. Helmeted heads peered down. A wire basket on a cable was lowered toward them for Pua. Josh and Tank leaped to steady the basket as it settled on the narrow path.

* * *

Nearly a month later, Josh and Tank slipped out of their zoris* and left them, in Oriental fashion, outside the Ladds' second-story Honolulu apartment door.

"I'm glad your dad's home again," Josh said.

"Yeah, but if Pua's father hadn't allowed the Coast Guard helicopter to take Dad off with Pua, the doctors say he'd have lost his leg to that coral-cut infection."

"I wonder how Pua's doing?" Josh mused, heading barefooted across the off-white living room rug.

"The last time we talked, she said she'll have only a few scars from the Toilet Bowl, and she promised to keep in touch." Tank padded past the tropical-print rattan couch and three matching occasional chairs in the living room. He opened the screen to the small lanai* that faced Diamond Head.*

In the kitchen, Josh removed two cans of soft drinks from the refrigerator and rejoined his friend. "Well, at least we know that they caught Maka, and he didn't have rabies. So nobody had to take the shots."

Tank accepted a cold can and popped the top. "I'm glad that the authorities took the cats and birds to quarantine." He shuddered, adding, "I'm especially glad they caught that big snake."

"They also destroyed those pokololo plants and removed the booby traps."

The phone rang. Josh carried his can of soda inside and picked up the receiver. "Hello, Josh Ladd speaking."

A girl's voice said, "This is Pua. Remember me?"

"Of course! Tank and I were just talking about you. How's everyone?"

"Everyone's fine—Keoni, the sergeant, and me."

"And your father?"

"That's why I called. The hospital doctors say it'll take time, but he's going to be well."

"No more of sometimes thinking he's Captain Kidd?"

"No more. They think he'll even give up being a bush vet to stay with Keoni and me. We'll be a real family."

"That's wonderful, Pua!"

"I'm sorry Daddy gave you and Tank such a bad time."

"That's okay. Tank told me that he's learned forgiveness and understanding because of what happened. And my trust in God was strengthened through the testing in that experience. Oh, sometimes I had my doubts while it was happening, but I never gave up. Now I feel more confident about trusting God."

"That's good. Oh, another reason I called," Pua continued, "is that I wanted to thank you for thinking of the rope and the oil back there when I was drowning."

"I got the idea after Tank and I went in with you and Keoni the first time. I had a plan in case it ever happened. I'm just glad I was there to help."

"So am I." The girl paused, then added, "Our grand-mother says she'd like you, Tank, and your families to come to a real Hawaiian luau* to celebrate when Daddy gets out of the hospital."

"We'd be glad to come," Josh assured her.

After Pua and he had said goodbye, Josh rejoined Tank on the lanai and repeated his phone conversation.

Tank commented, "Everything ended well, but I don't ever want to have another adventure like that."

"I don't either, yet I'd hate to lead a dull life. So would you, if you'll just admit it."

"Maybe you're right. I know we'll have them as long as you're around. I wonder what'll happen next?"

Josh grinned at his friend. "I can hardly wait to find out!"

Tank groaned in mock dismay, then returned the grin. "I hate to admit it, but—me too! Me too!"

End

GLOSSARY

Chapter Two

Bush Vets: A term applied to military veterans, especially of the Vietnam War, who shun society and generally live solitary existences in the jungles and remote areas of Hawaii.

Pupule: (*poo-POO-LAY*) Hawaiian for crazy.

Lava tube: (*LAH-vuh tube*). Formed when melted rock or lava from a volcano hardens first on the outside, forming a crust through which the hot interior magma continues to flow. Eventually, most of the lava drains out of the inside, leaving a tube or tunnel.

Kilauea Iki: (*kil-AH-way-ah EE-kee*) Literally, "Little Kilauea." A small volcanic crater connected to the larger active volcano on the Big Island and known as Kilauea. That's the Hawaiian word for "spewing" or "rising smoke cloud."

Koolau Range: (*koh-OH-lau [as in ow!] range*) The volcanic mountains rising directly behind Honolulu.

Pokololo: (*poe-koe-LOE-LOE*) Hawaiian for marijuana, a member of the hemp family. Marijuana is an illegal plant which is dried and used as a drug.

Punji Stick: (*pun-gee*) A piece of bamboo with sharpened point set at a 45-degree angle and concealed in grass or weeds to inflict leg and foot wounds on unsuspecting passersby, usually enemy soldiers.

'**Nam:** Contraction for South Vietnam, an Asian country where United States military forces suffered their only defeat in history. Americans were deeply divided over prolonged involvement in this conflict, which ended in 1973.

Chapter Three

Pot: Slang expression for marijuana, an illegal plant which is dried and used as a drug.

Pua: (*POO-ah*) Hawaiian for flower or blossom.

Keoni: (*kee-OH-nee*) Hawaiian for John.

Banyan tree: (*BAN-yun tree*): A member of the mulberry family that extends roots from its branches. These roots drop to the ground and form many secondary supporting trunks. A single banyan tree may cover several acres of ground.

Lei: (*lay*) Necklace of flowers which are given to people on arrival to Hawaii and sometimes on departure. Also worn for special occasions in the islands.

Hapahaole: (*HAH-pah-HOW-lee*) Hapa means half or part, so this is a person who's part Caucasian or white, and part nonwhite, as Hawaiian.

Oahu: (*Oh-WHA-hoo*) Hawaii's most populous island and the site of its capital city, Honolulu.

Ti: (*tee*) A plant with long, slender, green leaves that are used for many purposes in Hawaii. That includes skirts for the hula dancers who entertain visitors to the islands. Although many Mainlanders and songs refer to the dancers wearing "grass skirts," the skirts are usually made from ti leaves.

Tutu: (*too-too*) Hawaiian for grandmother.

Huhu: (*hoo-hoo*) Hawaiian for angry.

Chapter Four

Lafitte, Jean: (*zhan lah-FEET*). A French privateer who operated off the American coasts in the early 1800s.

Booby trap: (boo-bee-trap) Originally meaning a hidden explosive set off by an unsuspecting person moving a seemingly harmless object, the word has also come to mean any device that will harm an unwary person.

Chapter Five

Mongoose: A small, agile carnivore imported to Hawaii from India long ago. It feeds mostly on birds' eggs and rodents.

Kauai: (*COW-eye*) An Hawaiian island northwest of Oahu (where Honolulu is located.) Kauai is thought by many to be the most photogenic of the islands.

Hanauma Bay: (*ha-NOW-mah*) A picturesque and popular state underwater park located east of Honolulu.

Koko Head: A 646-feet-high extinct volcano and well-known landmark east of Diamond Head on Oahu.

Chapter Six

Kukui: (*coo-COO-ee*): The official tree emblem for the State of Hawaii, it's also called candlenut tree. Kukui trees are easily recognized by silvery green foliage. The oily nut kernels were used for candles or lights by early Polynesians. The nuts also make popular leis.

Mo'o: (*MOE-oh*) Hawaiian for lizard.

Chapter Seven

Poncho: (*pon-CHOH*) A garment like a blanket folded in the middle with a hole for the head, leaving the arms free. Military ponchos, with a hood added, use a water-repelling material to keep wearers dry.

Mauna Loa: (*mau-NAH loe-AH*): One of the state's two highest mountains (13,796 feet) and an active volcano. Mauna is Hawaiian for mountain. Loa means big or great.

Kailua-Kona: (*ky-LOO-ah KOH-nah*): An important community on the leeward (west) side of the Big Island.

Naalahu: (*Nah-ah-lah-hoo*): A community near the southern tip of the Big Island of Hawaii.

Guava: (*GWAW-vah*) A sweet yellow fruit growing wild in tropical areas, and common in Hawaii.

Lilikoi: (*LEE-LEE-coy*) Hawaiian for edible passion fruit.

Haole: (*HOW-lee*) An Hawaiian word originally meaning "stranger," but now used to mean Caucasians, or white people.

Chapter Eight

Piranhas: *(per-Rhan-yehs):* Small, vicious South American schooling fish known for attacking and devouring larger animals and even people.

Papaya: *(pa-PIE-ah)* A large, oblong, yellow fruit common in Hawaii.

Mango: *(man-GO)* A yellowish-red tropical fruit and the evergreen tree that bears it.

Feral: *(fher-l)* Not domesticated, as an animal that has returned to the wild or is descended from tame ancestors.

Basalt: *(bah-SAHLT)* Dense black rock produced by intense heat, as from a volcano.

Kiawe: *(kee-AH-vay)* A very thorny algaroba or mesquite tree that grows mostly in dry area. Kiawe may reach 60 feet in height.

Chapter Ten

Alii: *(Ah-lee-HEE)* Hawaiian word for native royalty.

Tapa: *(TAP-ah)* A fabric made from a tree bark and originally known by the Polynesian word, "kapa."

Chapter Eleven:

Lariat: *(LAIR-ee-et)* A lasso or long rope with a loop at the end used to catch livestock.

Malihini: *(mah-lah-HEE-NEE).* Hawaiian for newcomer.

Chapter Twelve
Taro: (*TAR-oh*) A plant grown throughout the tropics for its edible, starchy roots, and very popular in old Hawaii.

Chapter Thirteen
Volcanologist (*vol-CAN-ol-o-gist):* A person who scientifically studies volcanoes

Trust in the Lord... Proverbs 3:5-6 reads: "Trust in the LORD with all your heart, and lean not on your own understanding; in all your ways acknowledge Him, and He shall direct your paths." (NKJV)

Chapter Fourteen
Lilia: (*LEE-lee-ah*): Hawaiian for lily.

Chapter Fifteen
Hyperventilating: (*HIGH-per-VEN-til-a-ting*) Very fast, deep breathing that causes a decrease in the amount of carbon dioxide in the blood.

Zoris: (*ZOR-eez*) Flat, thonged sandals usually made of straw, leather, or rubber.

Lanai: *(LAH-nye*): Hawaiian for a patio, porch or balcony. Also, when capitalized, Lanai is a smaller Hawaiian island.

Diamond Head: An ancient volcano that collapsed upon itself to form Honolulu's most famous landmark.

* * *